DRAGON'S WISH

RED PLANET DRAGONS OF TAJSS BOOK THIRTEEN

MIRANDA MARTIN

CONTENTS

ADDISON

I look up, pushing my hair back off my face, and, as expected, my eyes immediately find Melchior. It's like they can't help but go to him whenever he's around. It's been that way ever since he came from the Tribe's caves to help.

The muted light in the makeshift lab we've put together reflects from his bronze-colored scales, the slight shimmer to them eye-catching on its own. It highlights his handsome face, with that strong jaw and broad forehead. It shines off his thick, dark hair and gilds the arc of his wings and his powerful tail.

I can't see the bright emerald of his eyes from this far away, just the dark fans of his lashes, but I know how mesmerizing they are against his tan skin and dark hair. That face doesn't take away from his impressive musculature either, accentuating the curve of his biceps, his pecs, those abs...

Feeling a flutter of reaction, I look away before he can catch me mooning over him like a schoolgirl. I try my best to refocus on the meteorite glass, which is what I'm supposed to be working on despite my wandering eyes.

All right.

Focus on the glass, not the hot dragon man, Addison.

It's easier said than done, but I need to finish the work. There have been some snags with the ancient technology shields that protect the city, and we need to figure out how to fix them.

I work for maybe ten minutes before my eyes wander over to Melchior again, watching as he frowns, focused on his own task. Why do I find that so adorable? He's proven himself to be a quick study, and the clear indication of his intelligence makes him even more intriguing. Damn it. I rip my eyes away and look down determinedly once more. I don't want to screw this up and make a mistake because I'm staring at Melchior.

I worked in the lab on the ship, and that knowledge has proven to be extremely valuable while we try to figure out this tech here on Tajss. And I have to say, I really like feeling like I'm important here in some way, like I'm needed. Maybe that sounds lame, but I'm not afraid of facing how I feel, even when I know exactly why I feel that way. It isn't a mystery.

I haven't felt important and needed very often in my life, not counting the brief time when I was a small child who was the apple of her father's eye. Right up until he left, of course.

My hands tighten at that thought, gripping the glass too firmly. Dangerously tight. I force myself to loosen my hold, shaking my head at myself. There's no point in focusing on past hurts. It does no good.

At least the painful memory succeeds in wiping away thoughts of Melchior just long enough that I fall back into the problem in front of me.

The meteorite glass has been working in the old Zmaj technology still here in the city, which is great. The problem is that we soon figured out it can't hold a charge for a longer duration. Which means if we use it as-is, the shields could very well fail at the worst time.

With the threat of the alien invaders always looming . . . yeah. We need to fix the issue ASAP.

When my hands cramp from using the small tools I need for the job, I straighten up again, shaking them out.

And, as I could have predicted, my eyes take the opportunity to seek out Melchior once more. He's still working diligently, his focus quite impressive. I wonder if he focuses on other things just as well...

"Addison?"

I jerk guiltily, turning towards Errol. I know I'm blushing, but there's no way I can control that.

"Yes?" I ask, hoping he doesn't realize I was staring at Melchior. Daydreaming. At least he isn't privy to some of my more X-rated thoughts.

"Any progress?" he asks, looking up from his own work. Good—he wasn't looking at me.

"No," I report glumly. "It still won't hold a longer charge."

"I have not made much progress either," he admits. "Perhaps it is better that we stop for the day and return tomorrow. Hopefully with a clear mind and a fresh perspective. We might be missing something because we have just spent too long staring at the problem."

I nod. That makes a lot of sense. Brain fatigue on something like this is definitely a thing.

"Okay." I look over at Melchior, feeling that familiar awareness, but hoping it isn't as obvious as it feels. "Melchior and I are on collection duty today anyway."

Melchior nods, setting down his tools as well. "Indeed. We shall go collect more meteorite glass and think on this."

We leave the lab together. It's a little frustrating that my stomach still fills with butterflies when he's nearby, even though we've worked in close proximity quite a bit at this point. But my body doesn't seem to care, doesn't seem to ever get used to him.

I look over at him discreetly before shifting my attention away. At least there's more to look at out here. The city itself is quite an impressive sight. I remember just how stunned I was when we first arrived, saw the technology the Zmaj had clearly been capable of building in the past, despite their much more primitive lifestyle now. The Devastation set their civilization back generations. Even now, I take the time to admire the city while passing through it, despite the fact that I live here.

"Do you think there is a solution that would result in the glass holding a longer charge?" Melchior asks as we walk through the city, heading for the desert outside its limits.

"I hope so," I say cautiously, sneaking a glance up at his face. The Zmaj are all over seven feet, so I have to look up quite high. When I see his eyes focused on me, I quickly face forward once more. "I don't want to stop trying yet."

We need it to work. We're outnumbered already and without the advantage of reliable shields-- yeah, not good.

"Yes," he replies as we near the border of the city. "I agree. I simply hope we will find a solution before there is another attack." He sighs. "Though perhaps we should discuss something else. I am certain Errol would chastise us for continuing to speak of it when we need to think of other things to gain the perspective he mentioned," he comments dryly.

I chuckle, nodding as I take one of the bins stacked at the edge of the city, put there specifically to collect more meteorite glass.

"You're probably right. How was the hunt you went on yesterday?"

"Ah." He grabs a bin as well. We could carry a bunch out there, but it's difficult to carry more than one back at a time.

They're unwieldy and heavy to boot. "The hunt was success-ful, even though we were tracking only one guster and came across three in total."

"Three?" I squeak, my mind flashing back to the guster attack on our party when we first landed here on Tajss. The giant lizard-like monster creatures were no joke. They killed many people right in front of me. "You killed all of them?" I ask incredulously.

He shakes his head.

"No, only two. And I was not alone," he adds as we step onto the sand and start walking out to where a group is already hard at work collecting glass.

"Oh, you're right—two isn't impressive at all," I scoff as I trudge through the sand. "Heck, I could take one down with a hand tied behind my back!"

He laughs, his emerald eyes twinkling as he looks down at me in appreciation.

"Perhaps you could," he murmurs, the admiration clear in his eyes.

Oh . . . I feel a flash of warmth at the look. That's really sweet, while also completely preposterous. I don't know quite how to respond. Does he have feelings for me too? Or is he just being friendly? Ugh, why is this so confusing! Luck-ily, I don't have to scramble for a response as we reach the others and they call out greetings. I'll take the distraction, thank you very much.

Both the humans and the Zmaj are on the schedule to gather more glass, but currently there are only Zmaj out here under the blazing hot suns. Not that they feel the heat in the same way we do.

Without the epis plant that they gave us to adapt to the climate here, we wouldn't have even survived, at least not above ground and definitely not in good health. Even under-ground, we didn't do well without it.

Doesn't mean the heat isn't still killer though. Needless to say, I don't love being out here in the desert, but I want to pull my weight. We all need to work hard to ensure our survival. And I'm actually relieved to have a task to do around Melchior so I don't make a complete fool of myself.

Lucky for us, the meteor showers have been relatively frequent, so there is quite a bit of glass to be had. We need a lot of it both for experimentation and to run the tech in the city. Apart from its utility, the glass itself is beautiful, smooth and black, and it reflects the light in a rainbow of colors. I can see why Kate adorned her bridal gown with bits of it. When the meteorites hit the sand, they melt it, creating the resource naturally at the bottom of the craters. After we discovered it had the electromagnetic properties needed to power the Zmaj machinery, we went into collection mode full force.

I survey the pockets of it as I pull on my protective gloves. Crouching, I tug a piece up and slide it gently into the bin I set down next to me. I don't want to break the bigger pieces. We might have to anyway to get them to fit certain space restrictions in the various pieces of tech, but I want the option of keeping them large just in case.

Melchior settles his bin near mine and gets to work as well.

Yes, I watch him.

But, in my defense, I don't really have to think a whole lot for this task, so I can watch and pick up glass at the same time. What an accomplishment. I'm such a role model.

"How are you liking the city so far?" he asks as we continue to work side by side.

"It's great," I answer truthfully. "Way better than the tunnels we were in before we stumbled across Errol. And the epis is a lifesaver. Not to mention there's so much technology to play with here!"

Melchior nods, a smile tugging at his full mouth. "Yes, that is true."

"What about you?" I prod, wiping at the sweat already accumulating on my upper lip. It's basically impossible to stay looking cute in this heat. And when did I start worrying about stuff like that? "Do you like visiting the City? I know your Tribe lives a day or so way from here in caves."

I'm really curious about that. Before we crash-landed on Tajss, the Zmaj were living much more of a hunter-gatherer lifestyle. None of them really stayed together much because of the bijass, their word for the male aggression instinct they find hard to control around each other. But somehow the members of what they call the Tribe made it work.

He looks toward the city, silhouetted against the red Tajss sky. It's an impressive sight.

"I suppose," he admits, still staring. "Familiarity with it is growing, the oddity of it fades the more time we spend here." He shrugs, going back to gathering glass. "With the threat of the invaders, the many humans who live here need the protection it can provide."

That's true, the majority of the surviving human population lives here. There are two other settlements with people who chose not to live in the city with us. The Tribe, where Melchior is from, was established way before humans even got here, so I understand their desire to continue to live separately.

But I really don't get the mining settlement. Those people know they need our help, need Zmaj help, but their own xenophobia made them pull away. The one good thing that has come from the invader attacks is that the disparate factions have realized just how vulnerable they are and have come to the table to work together, even if it is in a small capacity only involving the Zmaj as guards.

That inroad could lead to more of an alliance later, which

is something at least. It's more than Rosalind was apparently able to get for a while.

"I wonder if—"

"What do you think you are doing?"

The loud, threatening voice cuts our conversation short. I turn towards it. Melchior is already taking a step forward next to me.

"What's going on?" I ask him in a low voice.

Ryuth and Astarot are snarling at each other now, starting to circle.

Shit. This can't be good.

"The bijass. They are having trouble controlling it," Melchior explains grimly. "Stay back."

I nod, having no intention of getting any closer to the potential fight.

The bijass. That primal part that lives in all the Zmaj. I don't really understand it, but it's territorial and jealous and it makes them so aggressive they'll fight without being able to stop.

Melchior starts to walk towards them, his eyes sharp, his body tense as he nears, but Ryuth jumps Astarot before he can reach them.

I wince as they roll on the ground, the sound of blows and grunts of effort loud in the silence. At least neither of them has his lochaber in hand. That would have really upped the chance of one of them getting seriously hurt. Metal-tipped spear injuries are no joke.

My heart rises in my throat as Melchior approaches, no hesitation in his step when he grabs Ryuth and yanks him away from his opponent.

Ryuth shrugs him off and turns with a snarl.

"Together we are stronger!" Melchior admonishes sharply. His voice is deep and commanding, the order in them clear.

I hold my breath, watching the two combatants. Will he be able to get through to them?

The tension rises while we wait to see.

Then Ryuth growls, "survival of the group matters," before spinning away from Melchior and stalking off. I don't know where he's going. But some distance does seem like a good idea.

I let out the breath I was holding.

Astarot takes a few deep breaths, lying on the sand.

Melchior walks over, holding out a helping hand that the other Zmaj takes after only a brief hesitation. He pulls Astarot to his feet, and then the two look at each other.

Melchior's control, his tight focus, is clear even from this far away. He is powerful in his own right, but his ability to keep that tight lid on himself is one of the reasons the other dragons respect him so much.

Astarot is no exception. After a few seconds, he nods to Melchior, turning to get back to work.

Crisis averted, at least for now. I feel my own respect and admiration for Melchior rise. There aren't a whole lot of people who could have broken up that fight with as little fuss as he did. And as he stands there, framed by the sun behind him, his muscled body straight and tall, his eyes watchful as he scans the area...

I wonder what it would be like to be with someone like that. Someone so strong, so completely in charge of himself. What would it be like to actually date a dragon? I find myself thinking about it more and more.

Movement in the corner of my eye signals someone approaching—Visidion, crests a nearby dune. He must have gone out further to harvest the glass that isn't so near to the city and heard the scuffle. He slides down the dune in a controlled movement that I could never hope to emulate, his gaze going to Melchior.

His eyes then go to Ryuth, whose back is turned to us while he walks off his anger, before they shift over to Astarot, who is digging up meteor glass with much more fervor than is strictly required.

Visidion's shoulders relax as he turns to walk over to Melchior, the situation apparently under control.

Then Ryuth turns around, rage still clear on his face as he stalks back towards us.

I'm not the only one who sees it.

Before Visidion can reach Melchior, he turns back around and takes a few steps to reach me.

"Addison, I think it's best you go back into the city. We will carry the bins that have been filled."

He's talking to me, but his eyes are on Ryuth, as are Melchior's. I'm no idiot. There's no reason for me to stay if it's dangerous. And they have this. They don't need me to help. They'll just worry that I'll be hurt in any fight that might happen, which could only distract them.

"Okay," I agree readily, hoping it doesn't come to a physical altercation before the two of them can get things back under control. "Thanks."

I make my way back to the city. We're still close enough that I don't feel vulnerable going back by myself. Once past the city limits, I nod at people, some I recognize, many more I don't.

I sigh as I reach my apartment and open the door to go inside, ready to clean myself up. I guess it isn't really that much of a mystery why I want Melchior. I admire his intelligence, how much in control he is in every situation, how he can hold a conversation. I guess it really is less about the package and more about who he is as a person. Not that the pretty package isn't also intriguing.

In any case, I go about the rest of my evening, cleaning up, eating at the communal dining hall, and then I come back to my place to go to bed. And I'm still thinking about Melchior as I close my eyes.

I sigh, turning over to my side. This is pretty damn pathetic. I'm embarrassed for myself.

Eventually, sleep does take over, despite my thoughts.

When I wake up the next morning, I'm determined to put Melchior out of my mind and focus on something productive. I have some spare time, so I decide to work on the alien writs that we captured from the invaders' ship near the mining settlement. I grab a quick breakfast and then head over to the area that I have set up just outside the lab.

The writs aren't our first priority, so I've been working on them sporadically, here and there when I have the time. The puzzle they represent is both fascinating and frustrating. The only references I have to work with are the old scraps of pre-Devastation Zmaj texts we found around the city.

The problem is, while the writing in the book looks like it's perhaps closely related to the Zmaj text, it doesn't quite match. And, even apart from the trouble I'm facing decrypting the writings, it's also puzzling how close the language seems to be to the salvaged Zmaj writing we've found.

Why are they similar at all?

The invaders' technology is so different from the low-functioning tech we've found inside the city.

Why would the language have anything in common, let alone be close enough that I could even consider using it as a reference?

It really is a mystery.

But I've always been up for a challenge. Particularly a difficult one. So I continue to beat my head against it, flipping through the book, going line by line, word by word. I don't make a heck of a lot of progress, but I knew going in that it would likely be a slow process, made even slower because I can't devote the bulk of my time and energy to it.

I have my chin braced on my hand as I stare down at the open book in front of me when Melchior arrives.

"Have you been able to decipher anything?" he asks.

I immediately straighten, smoothing down my hair.

"Not really," I admit as he steps closer. He stops right next to me, where I can feel the presence of his body as he looks down at the alien book.

As usual, I feel that prickle of awareness across my skin at his proximity. I want to close that couple inches of distance left between us. But I'd rather not make a fool of myself, so I don't.

"I can see why," he murmurs. "I haven't seen anything like these writs before." His attention turns to me. He's so close that I can see that special glimmer in his emerald eyes that never fades away. Maybe it's fanciful thinking, but I feel like it's just the force of his personality shining out. "Please let me know if there is anything I can do to help."

I nod enthusiastically, feeling a little bit like a dummy.

"Thank you," I say, my voice coming out a little squeaky.

I mentally slap myself. With a slight smile and a nod, he turns to leave, perhaps going back to the lab. I slump over again, watching his back as he leaves. Fine. Maybe I'm watching his ass as he leaves. Sue me!

I sigh once he's out of sight and try to get back into the zone I need to be in to work on the book. It takes me a while.

I don't know what it is about him, but he calls to the woman that I've kept tightly caged inside me. And I don't seem to have much control over her.

2

MELCHIOR

*W*hen I leave Addison still studying the alien writs, my hearts are beating faster, my scales are more sensitive, my senses more aware. It is how I always feel when I am in her presence, or when I even think of her. It is distracting to say the least.

When I get back into the lab to work a bit more with the meteorite glass, I cannot fully focus on the task at hand. Thoughts of her keep invading, which is not an unusual occurrence at this point. When Ladon enters the lab looking for me, I welcome the distraction.

"Melchior—are you available for an extra patrol around the city? One of the others needed to tend to another matter."

"Of course," I respond, already walking towards him.

"Excellent. Thank you," he says, his face brightening. "Now I do not have to keep circling the city to find someone to do the job."

I chuckle, walking out with him. The city is quite large. The task of searching to find various people would be rather irritating.

When we part ways outside, my smile slowly fades. All

has been eerily quiet since the last attack. None of us want to be caught off guard again, which is why we have been very strict about the patrolling around the city. If there is danger approaching nearby, we will see it coming.

At least the city has proper shielding, unlike the Tribe and the mining settlement. I frown as I step out into the sand outside the city limits, using my wings to give my body lift so I can skim across it rather than sink. The lackluster performance of the shields has me and everyone else on high alert.

Despite our hopes, currently they are still only makeshift half-protections. No one is sure if they will be sufficient over a long period. I hope we can solve the issue with the meteorite glass, but until then, those shields are the best we have. It is a far from ideal situation.

What if the asteroids stop raining down on Tajss? We will have only the glass we are now gathering. And if the glass needs to be continuously replaced because it cannot hold a charge, we will surely run out of the resource—too quickly for my own peace of mind at this rate. Or anybody else's.

I am staunchly opposed to becoming "sitting ducks" as the human females say. It is why we are working so diligently to find a solution. Though I have to admit, at least to myself, that the worry about the shields is not my only reason for being in the city. I have been deliberately volunteering for any job or mission that will bring me here, and I know exactly why.

Addison's pretty face flashes in my mind's eye.

Shining, light brown hair falls straight to her shoulders, framing her delicate face, dominated by her large, dark eyes. They've always looked mysterious and intelligent, as if she knows something she is not saying. She is not particularly tall for a human female, though I suppose they all appear short to me. Nor does she attempt to stand out in the way she presents herself.

My eye is still drawn to her.

She spends much of her time by herself, working in the lab and on the technology in the city. Her knowledge and expertise have been a wonderful addition, and I have not been able to stop thinking of her since I first saw her—just as my thoughts continue to circle around the female now.

How she bites her lip when she is concentrating on a particularly difficult problem. The way her face lights up when she speaks about a subject she is passionate about. She does not love large gatherings and often prefers spending time with herself in her living quarters or the lab. And unlike some of her human female counterparts, she is not prone to wearing form-fitting clothing that shows off her curves or to fixing her hair in intricate styles. She does not emphasize her femininity, focusing on the business at hand.

There is no way to truly hide that she is feminine. It is in the way she moves, her hips swaying from side to side gracefully. The way she holds her tools, her long slender fingers working with the utmost delicacy, the grace of her wrists anything but masculine. It is in the softness of her face...her skin...

At night, when I am alone, I often wonder if her skin feels as soft as it appears, if her hair is as silky as it looks. If she is as soft and delicate everywhere.

I imagine stripping her naked, pulling off the loose clothes she favors to reveal the woman's body underneath. Cupping the curves of her breasts, which I have heard rumors are not protected and tucked away like our females' breasts were, but soft and exposed. I want to slide my hands down the length of her shapely legs, want to kiss my way from her ankles all the way to—

The ground gives way underneath me.

I gasp as I fall into an old zemlja tunnel, plummeting

hard, scraping against the side of it, my hands burning as I scrabble for purchase in a vain attempt to stop my fall.

I curse at myself for being so distracted by fantasies of a woman I have no claim to that I completely missed the signs of the tunnel. My fellow Zmaj would laugh to see me now.

I grunt when I hit the ground with a good amount of force, the tunnel not wide enough for me to spread my wings and slow my descent that way. I bend my knees to absorb the impact.

I am not alone.

The rustling is the first sign, then the distinctive flapping of wings.

Oh no.

I cover my face as a cloud of sismis erupts, the entire nest boiling into the air from where they were hanging upside down above, their leathery wings making a distinct rustle that has the hair at the back of my neck standing on end.

They screech, the sound sharp and echoing as they dive at me, a swarm punctuated with fangs and razor-edged claws.

They are mostly scavengers, but the large groups they hunt in are dangerous to any living creature. And this is a large nest. They are a necessary part of Tajss, their dung fertilizing the ground in these zemlja tunnels so that epis, the plant that helps sustain our lives and the lives of the humans, can grow and flourish. Their claws are also quite useful, a key ingredient of the healing paste we use on wounds.

Their helpfulness is not quite at the forefront of my mind in this moment.

I crouch, using my lochaber to block the attacks and slice through the air around me, thick with the creatures.

I grunt as one sinks its teeth into my shoulder. I yank it off in a spray of my blood, snapping its neck and dropping it to the ground as I continue to defend myself against the rest. I remain low, knowing that I will encounter a lower density of the creatures here, though that does not mean I fully escape their bites and scratches.

I clench my jaw as I feel a particularly vicious raking along my back, twirling my lochaber to create a shield of sorts.

I cannot kill them all.

I must simply wait the creatures out. They were merely startled at my abrupt appearance and are attacking more because the opportunity presented itself than anything. If I kill enough of them, they will move on so I continue to stay low and attack the ones that venture too close.

As predicted, the crowd of the creatures around me gradually lessens as the group flies deeper into the tunnel. Soon enough, the air around me is completely clear.

I stay crouched low, taking deep breaths as I recover from the shock of falling and the fight itself.

This is a lesson for me.

When I finally straighten cautiously—how good it feels! —I can see the bodies littered around me, the light from above illuminating the carnage.

I look to my right, where the tunnel continues, the light shining only part of the way before it continues into a deeper black my eyes cannot penetrate. But I can hear the sound of the sismis flying farther and farther away. Good.

I turn back to the winged carcasses. Perhaps I can pull something positive out of this idiotic mistake. I pull off the empty pouch I keep tied to my waist just in case, then reach for the first body. It is still warm in my hands as I use my knife to cut off its claws, working quickly. The last thing I need is to linger here in this tunnel in case the sismis circle back. Or, even worse, if I am wrong about the age of the tunnel and there are still zemlja here.

The massive tunneling creatures are also necessary for

the epis we require, but they are a far greater threat than the sismis.

I work quickly, declawing each of the creatures and slipping the harvest into my pouch to use for a healing paste when I return home. I finish fast, clean the blood from my hands and tools the best I can, and turn to the opening. I scan the way I fell and see the tunnel does not come straight down, which is good, because it will be easier to climb out.

Crouching down low, I push up hard with my legs, leaping as far as I can before I have to dig my hands and feet into the rock and sand, sliding part-way down as I do. The climb is not easy, but I make progress, sliding back occasionally but continuing to move forward despite the small setbacks.

When I finally reach the opening at the top, I haul myself out and inhale deeply, sitting down to catch my breath. I look down at the deep hole beside me. I will not allow myself to be so distracted again. It has proven to be quite dangerous. I check myself. All the wounds I sustained are minor.

Sighing, I stand, flicking the sand off myself before I continue on the rest of the patrol. Luckily, I do not encounter any more danger for the rest of it.

On my sweep back around the city, my mind is clear and focused. Then I look over at the city and my gaze stops on a familiar figure.

Addison.

My forward momentum falters, and I slow despite myself. She is speaking with Rosalind, the human female in charge of the city. Tall, with long hair and a powerful feminine frame, the Lady General is quite a contrast to Addison, who is smaller, her clothing more inconspicuous, her frame not as large. I know many would look at Rosalind first. But she does not draw my attention as Addison does.

Her quiet beauty, her fascinating mind...all of her tugs at

me in a place that has long been dormant, asleep. There is so much of the past I do not remember, an issue I know many of my brethren face as well, our minds attempting to protect us from the trauma of the Devastation, the cataclysmic war that destroyed our civilization. But something about Addison tugs at those buried secrets in a way I have not experienced before.

I linger even though I know I should leave, my eyes hungrily tracing the delicate lines of her face, watching as she gestures with those slender, clever hands. I could watch her for hours, though the opportunity to do so unnoticed does not often present itself. Even now, I see her shoulders tense somewhat and her head start to turn towards me.

She senses me.

I feel a warm glow at that fact. I have realized that she often knows I am in the vicinity, as if she might be as aware of me as I am of her. Though I do not know if she feels quite the same way. I do not know if her skin also feels too sensitive, her body overheated, at my proximity.

My own passion is distracting in its strength, awakening with a rush after a long slumber. I look away and continue forward before she turns fully towards me.

I do not want to scare her away with the intensity of my desire for her.

3

ADDISON

*T*he problem with the charge in the glass is getting to the point that I dream about it, think about it while eating, showering... Basically all the time. I glare down at the piece in front of me, suppressing the urge to just pick it up and throw it against the wall. All that will do is bring us down one piece of glass and make a mess I'll have to clean up. Damn it.

I scrub at my face. Okay, maybe it's time to take a step back for a few minutes. So I literally do just that. Take a long step back.

Just in time for Melchior to walk in with a bin full of more of the glass. He nods at me as he walks over to set down his burden.

"Thank you, Melchior," Errol says, straightening on his stool, rolling his own shoulders. I know he's hitting the same wall I am, but he seems to be taking it a whole lot better. Probably I should be taking cues from him.

"The last meteor shower left quite a bit for us to collect," Melchior comments, letting go of the bin. "I predict there will be continuous deliveries for quite some time."

"That's good, considering we're no closer to a solution," I say, even as I feel that spine-tingling awareness of Melchior that never seems to lessen or go away.

He nods, his face sympathetic.

"Yes. But I know if anyone can find the solution, it is you, Addison."

I feel my face warm at the unexpected compliment.

"I'm trying," I murmur, ducking my head, pretending to focus on the piece of machinery in front of me. Ugh, why do I become this shy, stumbling girl in front of him? I'm usually at my most confident in the lab. I'm around technology here, safely ensconced in the world where I'm most comfortable, most confident in my knowledge. But every time Melchior shows up, I feel like my confidence level immediately regresses. It's really annoying.

I frown, stepping forward to fake-tinker with the parts in front of me.

Hmm.

Melchior does seem to be coming to the lab more and more often. In fact...lately he's been making the vast majority of the deliveries from the Tribe himself. Is it possible...he's doing so on purpose?

I glance over at him, only to catch him looking at me. He immediately looks away.

Huh.

Maybe...maybe he's interested in me too? I look back down, feeling a wave of heat flow through me just at the thought. I'm probably reading too much into it. Maybe he just likes the city. Or maybe he's the fastest or something and keeps being chosen for that reason, I don't know.

"Is there anything new you have tried since last we spoke?"

I jump a little at Melchior's voice, unexpectedly close

now. My body is so damn aware of him, an electrical current shoots right through me.

"Uh, well..."

I go off on my spiel, the familiar topic steadying me somewhat—thankfully. He makes some intelligent commentary, which is what I've come to expect from him now. The sound of his voice is both stimulating and calming at the same time. It has the kind of deep timbre that makes me feel safe. Stupid, but what about my reaction to the guy isn't?

We're still in the middle of our conversation, Melchior so close now that I can smell the distinctive scent coming off him, when Bashir walks in. I only glance at him, my focus almost fully on Melchior. He smells like the outdoors, but not in a bad way. The Zmaj don't sweat—I giant advantage, if you ask me. I feel like a soggy mess after I'm out in the desert for longer than five minutes.

"Have you made any progress?" Bashir asks, drawing my attention back to him despite myself.

"Nothing of note as of yet," Errol answers for the both of us. "But we are going to keep studying the matter."

Bashir nods, glancing at all the machinery we've already picked apart, pieces lying here and there. I suppose if you just walk in, it could look like a graveyard, somewhere tech might go to die, but it's actually quite organized, a method to what might look like madness to the untrained eye.

"One of the children had a dream last night," he murmurs, crossing his arms, his face thoughtful. "I think it is...interesting."

"Interesting?" Errol asks, putting down his tools to give Bashir his attention. "How so?"

Bashir frowns, looking over at Melchior and me as well. He has all of our attention by this point.

"It was a dream about Tajss," he explains. "Almost like it was...trying to communicate."

I share a glance with Melchior. Weird.

"What do you mean?" I ask carefully. "Like the planet itself was trying to speak to him?" I ask, half smiling at the thought already.

But Bashir doesn't crack a smile. In fact, he looks really serious when he shakes his head.

"Yes, exactly," he confirms with a straight face. "It is trying to tell us something. I believe...I believe it is attempting to prepare us, giving us what protection it can so we can fortify our defenses, prepare for the inevitable attack."

"You mean the asteroid showers," Errol says slowly. "You believe Tajss is responsible?"

"Yes. I do not think it is a coincidence that the showers started when they did. That they have appeared multiple times, right when we needed them to help repel an attack from those alien invaders. That the glass itself is a necessary component we need in order to resurrect our technology, including the shields that will hopefully help protect the Tribe and the mining settlement as well." He shakes his head. "My own experiences with Tajss lead me to believe it is sentient in its own right."

Errol does not appear to dismiss the thought immediately.

"That is a bold claim," he says slowly, tilting his head in consideration.

"Are you proposing we engage in some form of...planetary worship?" Melchior interjects. His tone and his skeptical expression speak for itself. "That is a dangerous road to embark upon. Religion is often a dividing force."

Bashir meets Melchior's eyes, not at all irritated at the push back, but Melchior's skepticism isn't shaking what he believes.

"I do not think anyone should do anything they do not feel comfortable doing," he states after a brief pause. "And I also do not see a reason that it is necessary we all think alike. I do not think that is healthy for our society. I am simply stating what I myself think is happening. You can agree. Or not."

With that closing salvo, he nods at all of us and leaves the lab, his information delivered.

I don't know how to feel here. I might not be quite as open as Errol on the subject...but I don't feel quite as skeptical as Melchior does either. I guess I'm more intrigued at the idea than anything. I've been agnostic for most of my life, ever since my father left us on Christmas day while we were still aboard the ship. I remember that dark time. A child simply does not have the capacity to process why a parent, a person that is supposed to love and care for you, would be so selfish as to leave when you most need him.

I felt lost and alone. Unwanted.

I didn't even know what my purpose was, any nascent belief I had in a higher power thoroughly shaken.

If a higher power existed, why would it let my father be taken away from me? It didn't make much sense, not to the child. And not to the adult now, really.

Luckily, I found some solace through another avenue. A teacher on the ship who was instrumental in teaching me about science, giving me a logical framework from which I could create a new inner sanctuary for myself. One I could count on. A place where facts reigned supreme and my emotions were safe, where they couldn't be sideswiped like they had been. Where the parameters for trouble were clear, where I could see it coming. Where I could solve a problem, or at least explain it using logic.

I appreciated that. Logic was something my household sorely lacked at the time. My mother was weak. I can see it clearly now that I'm an adult. She found the idea of being a single mother incredibly embarrassing, shameful even. Because of that tightly held belief, she did her best to hold onto the appearance of being happily married for much, much longer than she should have after my father left us. Until even she could no longer pretend that he would come back.

She never did take well to being a single parent. Her solution to the issue was often avoidance, in varying forms. One of her favorites was sleeping pills. She found solace in the pill bottle that she could not find in her real life, or in me, even though I so desperately needed her. That addiction took her from me far too often, forcing me to grow up way before my time. I became the housemaid and the cook whenever she went on one of her chemical trips. I remember coming home from school, my stomach in a knot as I wondered if I would find her passed out on the couch again, unresponsive to my attempts to wake her.

I never felt more alone than when she was there physically but gone in every way that mattered.

Still, as harsh as my childhood was, it also helped me grow strong quickly. I was mature and mostly independent at a young age. Those were traits that served me well in my professional life, if not my personal one.

But that's neither here nor there. The bottom line I guess is that I've been agnostic ever since. I don't know if there is a higher power, or powers for that matter.

Is it possible that Tajss is one? Considering the facts Bashir laid out so clearly...I'm not sure if he's that far off. That's not even considering the way he seems able to commune with the planet, or the dream he's saying one of the dragonlings had.

The meteor showers themselves make me think. And I've often wondered at Bashir's often uncanny intuition... What if telepathic communication with the planet is possible, like he asserts it is? Maybe there's a way to measure it, measure the planetary frequencies.

Maeve definitely experienced a telepathic link with Padraig after they were both marked with the asteroid glass...maybe there's something there... The thought works at the back of my mind as I continue to work in the lab for a bit longer.

And is the foremost thought there as I sit by myself during my lunch break. I wonder how I would go about exactly...

My train of thought derails as a familiar tingling sensation suffuses my body. Melchior. As if the thought of him summons him, he slides into the seat next to me.

"Hello, Addison," he murmurs, smiling at me as he sets his own food down in front of him.

"Hello," I return, smiling back as I force myself to take another bite of my food.

We're not in the lab now, nothing else to do with my hands but eat. I feel almost more naked, more vulnerable here than surrounded by the familiarity of the lab, my home away from home.

"What do you think about Bashir's theories?" he asks casually as he digs into his own food. "Do you believe there is any merit to them?"

I know he doesn't want to entertain them at all. But I'm not going to lie about what I think, no matter how much I like him, how much I'm attracted to him. Intellectual dishonesty is just not in my makeup. So I shrug.

"Anything is possible, right? Years and years ago, humankind thought our planet, Earth, was flat." I smile when Melchior chuckles at the thought. "Silly, I know. It didn't last. We studied the stars and eventually realized we could sail all the way around it. And then we went into space and actually saw that it was indeed spherical." I gesture around us. "We kept learning, kept adjusting what we thought we knew. And now here we are on Tajss. Light years away from what we used to believe."

Melchior nods thoughtfully. I can see he's considering his next words carefully. He meets my eyes. His are crystal clear, the green deep. Thoughtful. And completely mesmerizing.

"What do you believe in, Addison?" he asks softly, the words oddly intimate while people laugh and joke around us, eating their own lunch.

Too intimate. And they're touching on a somewhat sensitive subject for me.

I break eye contact, looking down at my food.

"I believe whatever science can prove," I return briskly. "Whatever I can see, touch, hear, measure. That's what I believe in."

A pause as I take another bite, chewing automatically.

"I respect that, " Melchior finally murmurs. "Requiring evidence keeps potentially dangerous illusions at bay."

I nod, considering the clear bias in those words.

Perhaps.

4

MELCHIOR

*T*he more time I spend around Addison, the more time I want to spend around her. Each time I see her, I can feel that initial attraction deepening, my affection for her growing. Perhaps I am making myself too vulnerable without knowing if she returns even a portion of my own feelings, but I cannot seem to help myself when she is the subject.

I know that she might be noticing that I am around her as much as I can be, attempting to do everything I can to be helpful whenever the need presents itself, whether she needs me to lift a heavy item or she needs me to escort her to the dining area.

Not that she needs an escort to the dining area—she is more than capable of going alone.

I just want to be around her as much as I can and being helpful seems like a good excuse. Perhaps a thin one at times, but it is the best I can come up with. I am not ready to reveal my feelings quite yet.

Addison is not only supremely independent, she is also deeply vulnerable. Perhaps it is odd to find those two qualities in such strength in the same person, but I know I am correct. I have spent much time with her at this point.

With my growing emotions comes an intense calling to protect her, heal whatever wounds she carries. The problem is, I am as of yet still uncertain exactly how much attention would be too much for this complex woman. I am still agonizing over the next step I should take as I hover in the lab, ready to lend a pair of helping hands. When she goes to pick up a bin full of glass, I am there before she can get a full grip on the thing.

"Allow me," I murmur. "Where would you like it moved?"

"Oh. Over there," she directs, smiling at me. "Thank you, Melchior."

I nod, hefting the box.

"Would you like these two moved there as well?" I ask, gesturing with my chin to the other two that were on the table next to the bin I already have.

"Oh, you don't have to get all of—"

"It is no trouble," I insist, walking over to deposit the bin, already coming back to pick up the others.

When an alien invader's body is dropped off in the lab, I pick it up and move it to where she wants it. I know this is not the first such body she has seen, but she still wrinkles her nose, obvious distaste in her expression as she nears it.

Textured blue skin shows where the body is unprotected —only the head, hands, and feet remain uncovered by the armor they wear. The eyes currently open and staring are completely black, with thick brow ridges above. The lipless mouth contains sharp teeth and a pair of tusks that curve out, almost touching in the front. It has six arms, three on either side of its torso, though only the ones in the center are large. They are the most functional, ending as they do with clawed three-fingered hands. The other four arms are smaller and thinner, ending in small pincers, most likely the reason for the emblem they wear, a stylized yellow pincer on a brown background. The matte brown carapace armor is a point of interest. Anything we can learn about their technology and defenses is knowledge that might aid us in the future.

"I know it's hot out there, but I wish they'd be able to get bodies to me faster," Addison mutters, her frown already fading as she studies the body. "They always have that smell of rotting fish..."

"The smell is...unpleasant," I agree.

"Hmm."

I watch as she cuts into the carapace, muttering to herself while she uses tweezers to pick up a small piece. When she tries to move the body, I am there to help.

"Would you like me to hold it on its side?" I ask politely, taking a firm two handed grip.

"Uh, yes. That would be great."

So I do just that.

And move some more heavy boxes.

And another body that comes in.

Perhaps it does not sound like the most exciting afternoon, but I am quite content simply spending time with Addison. She straightens from the machinery she went back to after working on the body, stretching with her hands pressing at the small of her back. I would love to rub out any knots or soreness she might have.

"I think it's time for a lunch break," she announces, turning towards the door.

"Take your time," Errol calls out, still focused on the part he is tinkering with. "You need the break."

"You're right," she agrees, taking a deep breath.

And stopping abruptly as I step into her path.

"I can escort you to the dining area," I offer, moving to her side.

She appears somewhat startled, blinking up at me for a moment in silence.

"Oh...uh...yeah, sure," she stammers out.

Perhaps not the best reaction, but I am happy to be at her side as we continue out and down to eat.

Eating with her has quickly become one of my favorite things to do. I have more time to simply speak with her, unlike in the lab where she often requires concentration to work. And that lunch is no exception.

"Have you learned anything more of the alien writs?" I ask, curious.

Her face grows animated, and she sets down the bite she was about to eat.

"Not yet, but I have to say, the more I dig into what we've found here in the city, the more fascinated I am..."

I watch her as she speaks. The expressions that cross her face, the way her eyebrows lift and lower, the movement of her hands. I really enjoy seeing her speak about something she is passionate about. And I also notice she is more relaxed around me now than she was in the beginning, especially if we speak about something she is working on. Perhaps we can move to more personal topics at some point, but I am happy to hear her views on her work as well.

"And how is the Tribe doing?" she asks halfway into our meal.

I sigh, turning my mind to the more serious topic.

"There are problems we are going to have to address," I admit. "Things have changed with the influx of more people and with the threat of off-worlders we are all worried about."

She nods, her expression turning sympathetic.

"Yeah, it feels like if it isn't one thing it's another," she sighs. "And I worry...that things might get worse before they get better."

I nod. I understand what she means. There are not so

many of us that every possible casualty will not be felt. If we are attacked and we lose people, yes, we would need fewer resources.

But we would be heartsick.

Every person we have is valuable, contributing in his or her own way.

When I excuse myself after lunch to go meet with Commander Visidion, I am still thinking of the threat we must prepare for.

"Melchior," he greets me warmly, clasping my arm and gesturing to the table. "Please, have a seat."

As the city has slowly become more of a home, small tables and chairs have begun appearing in various areas, places to sit outside. I appreciate the addition. Just as I appreciate being able to sit down indoors.

Visidion takes a seat across from me, his strong demeanor something I have always admired. He also has a way of focusing on a person that makes one believe you are the center of his universe, at least in that moment in time.

I will forever be grateful to have won a place among his most trusted, thankful to escape the fate of wandering the sands, lost to the bijass. The thought makes me shudder even now, even as we settle into our first topic.

The patrol routes.

"I want to make certain I am not overburdening anyone too much," Visidion remarks as we plan them. "I would like to have multiple patrol routes, reaching farther out into the desert, but that would require more Zmaj than I want to devote to the task with everything else we need to accomplish."

"We need more defenses for the Tribe," I agree. "Ones that do not necessarily require our physical prowess."

"Yes," Visidion agrees grimly. "Especially since the shields Errol has come up with are not yet guaranteed to work. We cannot depend on them, though I hope that changes in the future."

We discuss using different types of weapons—the sharpened poles the females came up with proved to be quite effective when the cave system was attacked.

We also discuss the possibility of another wall, creating a thicker buffer between the living spaces and the outside, among other possibilities.

"We will continue to discuss our defenses later, but we have to continue on to an equally pressing matter. The issue of the food supplies," Visidion continues. "We do not have enough stored. I do not like knowing that we are so close to disaster if there is an emergency of some sort."

I nod, sobering at the thought.

"Yes," I agree. "We have even more people now we need to feed and over hunting has reduced the game we can easily access." As a hunter for the Tribe, this is an issue that I am well versed on. "Perhaps we should put rules into place for the short term that only allow hunting farther away, so game may travel back to us. Hunting parties would need more time because more traveling would be required, but perhaps the burden of at least carrying the meat back can be eased using carts and other means of transport..."

I trail off as I see Addison walk by, speaking with another female.

I adore how she walks, the feminine sway of her hips, the way her shorter legs travel distance faster than she appears to be moving...

"Melchior." I jerk my attention back to Visidion to find him grinning at me, glancing over at Addison's figure before looking back at me. I feel the warm rush of embarrassment. I was not at all discreet about watching her. And Visidion is no fool. "I have not given you a night off of patrols in months. Why do you not take tonight to...pursue your own desires."

I stare back at him, stunned at both the time off and the odd directive tacked onto the end. This is unusual. I feel as though Visidion might be communicating something without saying it outright, and he appears much...warmer than usual.

Odd. Very odd.

"Uh...yes, that is very kind of you," I say, standing, ready to create some distance between myself and this alternate version of Visidion. "Thank you."

"Of course."

I can hear him chuckling behind me when I turn awkwardly and walk away quickly, as if he is savoring something particularly humorous.

5

ADDISON

I turn over once more, the sheets tangling around my legs. I've been tossing and turning for hours, unable to shut down my brain long enough to fall asleep. I flip over to my back with a sigh, staring up at the ceiling. I'm tired and I need sleep, but I can't shake the thoughts of Melchior that keep nagging at me. It's the way he's been acting, spending so much time around me, being so helpful whenever he's in the vicinity...I'm starting to suspect that he might share this attraction I feel for him.

Even apart from how much he seems to like to help me, he likes to spend lunch time with me, seeks me out for conversation. And the way he looks at me when he thinks I'm not watching....

I squeeze my eyes shut as that now-familiar tingle of arousal spreads through me. This is ridiculous. I'm not a teenager dealing with raging hormones. Get ahold of yourself, woman!

I don't have time for a distraction like this, but Melchior is like my kryptonite—my mind turns to mush around him, and thoughts of him plague me all the time. Even while I should be focused on the tasks in front of me, on the problems I need to study and fix for all of our sakes.

I don't have time for this!

I turn over to my other side, punching the pillow underneath me even though it's done absolutely nothing wrong. It just has the unfortunate luck of being right there when I need to vent.

Distractions are not what I need right now, but it really doesn't seem to matter. I've never had a problem focusing on work before, but I just can't pull my mind away from him. From his impressive musculature—broad shoulders, muscled arms and legs, his cut torso with that eight-pack, the hard curve of his butt—My fingers curl with the desire to touch all of that delicious body.

Then there are his eyes. I can't look into the emerald depths of his eyes for too long. I can feel myself sinking into them if I hold contact for too long. I avert my gaze regularly for just that reason. But all of that is physical. If it was just physical, maybe I would have a better handle on myself.

But it's not.

The more time I spend with him, the more impressed I am by his giant heart—well, his metaphorical heart. I know the Zmaj have two. So, giant hearts? I roll my eyes at myself. Either way, that empathy he has, that almost innocent masculinity that makes me feel like he'll always be watching over me, or anyone who needs help for that matter.

It's damn near impossible to resist. He's a hero, in the truest sense of the word. And not only in the way most if not all of the Zmaj are. His goodness goes deep down, right to the core of him.

It's who he is.

It's completely shaken my idea of men, like I've encountered something completely alien in him. Okay, that calls for another eye roll. Yeah, technically he is an alien, so I guess I should say he's a completely different type of male.

I still feel like he's the best man I've ever known, regardless of his genetics.

How far off are they really if we can procreate with them? I figure that makes them close enough that the comparison is fair. I know for a fact that it's changed my opinion of men for the better.

Nobody has ever made me lose sleep like this. I brood about that for some time. But, eventually, my body is so tired that I start to drift off despite myself. As tired as I am, I don't fall into a dreamless sleep like I usually do when I'm exhausted. That would be too easy.

Instead, Melchior manages to invade my dreams as well. Granted, it isn't the first time, but the dreams aren't...carnal like the ones I've had before. Although Melchior is featured prominently, they feel less romantic and more focused on Tajss.

I feel a sense of urgency, of need as I'm treated to a sweeping view of Tajss, of the endless red sand, the rocks, the gorgeous but relentless suns. And the wildlife indigenous here, from the ones that are familiar to me like the guster and vtak, to those I haven't seen before, fantastic creatures that are as alien as anything I might have seen in a science fiction movie.

Underground, in the sky, even in water, as rare as that is here. I'm filled with wonder at the vastness of the planet, at the amount of life I would not have expected given the desolate nature of this place.

I frown in my sleep as the wordless emotions grow. But the sense of wonder doesn't last. The images keep shifting, but the emotion with them changes.

It feels...dangerous?

The colors change, turning darker, the overall tone of the dream turning decidedly ominous. No more animals. Each image starts to linger for a longer period of time. Where before the landscape had a vibrant beauty to it, it now appears foreboding, the shadows longer and darker, an eerie stillness to everything.

I begin to feel vulnerable. Like prey knowingly waiting for a predator. I want to turn around, want to make sure nothing is creeping up on me from behind, but I can't. I'm not in charge of this dream.

My view switches to Melchior. I see him in various places. The city, what must be the cave system where the Tribe lives, the desert. I even see myself, which is really disorienting, even in the context of a dream, which I am aware this is. And then Melchior and me together with the red background of Tajss.

We're holding hands now.

Looking at each other.

And then, as one, both the figures turn to look at me. My eyes and his staring at me. The look in both is almost...pleading.

But I have the distinct feeling that the call for aid isn't from either Melchior or me. Something else is staring at me through our eyes. Something much more vast, something so totally different that I can only recognize it's some kind of consciousness, but beyond that...

I focus on Melchior's eyes, on the depth of the green in them, and I start to fall in, start to be sucked into the depths of them, and I can't pull back...

I wake with a jolt, a light layer of sweat covering my body, my breath coming fast, my heart rate elevated. I sit up, taking a deep breath as I push my damp hair off my face.

That was...something.

I glance at the clock. I've only slept for a few hours, but it's already time to get back up and get back to work.

The dream doesn't leave me as I clean up and grab some clothes to throw on. It didn't feel like a regular dream. The emotions were too intense, the images too clear and sharp. I think about that as I leave my quarters and head out to the lab, waving absently when people call out greetings.

"Good morning," I call out to Astarot when I step into the lab. He calls out his own greeting as I sit down at one of the tables.

My brain keeps working on the puzzle of the dream while I keep beating my head against the problem with the glass. While I work through the images, the emotions that bombarded me during the dream, I think it is a kind of message. But what kind?

First I saw the beauty of Tajss, the life here.

Then I saw the same Tajss, but with no life, the images somehow sinister. Like something terrible had happened?

And then Melchior and me holding hands, together. But it wasn't us either. Something else was behind our eyes, asking, pleading for something. Desperate for some kind of help.

Melchior and me together...

Maybe that Tajss needs help? And Melchior and I need to work together? I don't know if I'm interpreting everything correctly, but the more I think about it, the more convinced I am that it was a meaningful dream.

I look up when I hear someone else enter the lab.

It's Melchior.

Immediately, a bunch of questions flood my mind, but I look over at Astarot and hold my tongue. I might sound completely crazy peppering Melchior with questions about a dream I had.

"Morning," I murmur instead when Melchior greets me.

Then I pretend to get back to work. It really is pretending this time. I can't focus for the life of me. All I keep doing is replaying segments of the dream over and over again, trying to pick apart what each image might mean.

"Do you need help?" Melchior asks when I try to shift over a heavy part.

"Thank you—would you mind moving it to that end?"

He moves it, and I find myself watching him even more closely than I usually do, but it isn't just because he looks good anymore. Though he does, and I feel the same awareness of his physical proximity that I always do.

I don't know what I'm thinking really. Like maybe I might be able to glean some information from how he looks? That doesn't make a heck of a lot of sense, but I'm at my wits end here.

"Astarot—can I have a word with you?"

It's Visidion.

I feel myself tense as Astarot gets up and steps out with Visidion, leaving Melchior and me alone. I feel a rush of relief, opening my mouth to let loose about the dream.

Melchior beats me to the punch.

"Addison, you were in my dream last night."

I close my open mouth slowly as Melchior settles onto a stool next to me, his expression serious as he scans my face.

Questions flood into my mind. Is this a coincidence? What kind of dream? Did he feel the same emotions? I shake my head as they come one after another. I need to start at the simplest.

"I had a dream with you in it too," I admit, feeling a twinge of fear that I try to suppress. This could be nothing at all—I could be making something out of nothing at all. "What was yours about?"

It will probably be something like a typical dream, maybe

a random mix of scenes or events that don't really mean anything.

He frowns, propping his elbow up on the table.

"It began with pictures of Tajss. The landscape, the animals..."

I feel my stomach tighten, my heart sink. "But then it shifted?" I ask, my voice low. I almost don't want to know the answer.

He nods, the set of his mouth grim. "Yes," he agrees, his eyes searching my own. "The images grew darker. Desolate."

"Foreboding?" I ask, fear a steady threat inside me now.

His eyes grow even sharper as he watches me.

"Yes," he says slowly, tilting his head. "Addison...what happened next? I am starting to wonder if..."

"We had the same dream," I finish reluctantly. "On the same night." We're both quiet as we puzzle over that. "Fine. I'll finish it. Maybe we're making something out of nothing here—you tell me." He nods, his gaze watchful. "Okay. After the images change and the animals go away...I saw you. In different places—the city, at the Tribe's home, I think, in the desert."

"I saw you as well," he interjects. "In the city, the desert...and underground."

I feel a chill rush through me, the fine hairs on my arms standing on end.

"And then I saw both of us together. Holding hands," I continued, my throat clicking as I swallowed.

"When I saw our eyes...there was something else in them. Not us," Melchior finishes quietly, his gaze troubled. "It did not feel like a normal dream."

"No," I agree. "It didn't."

We both sit there, quiet.

"Did you...did you feel the emotion at the end?" I ask hesitantly. "Like it was a warning, finishing with a cry for help of some sort? Maybe?"

Melchior nods, even more reluctant than me.

"Their eyes...our eyes...they were asking for something. Perhaps you are right and it was aid."

I shake my head, frowning.

"The warning was about Tajss...is it possible that...Tajss is asking for help?"

It sounds crazy, even crazier said out loud than it did floating around in my head. How are we supposed to help Tajss? How could Melchior and I together possibly accomplish anything worthwhile for something so vast? Which also brings Maeve and Padraig to mind...is it possible Tajss brought them together? Just as it seems to be putting Melchior and me together now? Does the meteorite glass induce some kind of telepathy? Some kind of connection between mates maybe? I feel a thrill at the thought. And I feel my stomach roll simultaneously. I need to calm down.

There was nothing at all romantic about the dream, apart from us holding hands, which could easily be platonic, right?

"It feels like a dream calling us to some type of action," Melchior agrees grudgingly. It is obvious he is loath to come to that conclusion. "But I feel as though we need someone with more expertise to help us determine exactly what it is we think both of us dreamed."

"Bashir," I murmur. He definitely knows a lot more about this, about Tajss in particular.

"Yes. We need to speak with Bashir. Perhaps he can help us with this." He doesn't look at all happy about coming to this conclusion. I can completely relate. But he doesn't close his eyes to the matter or ignore it despite his reluctance. Something I can truly appreciate. "We need to go to the Tribe."

I nod, looking down. I feel completely out of my element

here. I don't deal with dreams and emotions. Facts and evidence are where I'm most comfortable. But it looks like I'm about to step right out of my comfort zone.

Hell—it looks like I'm about to be catapulted right out of it.

Whether I want to or not.

6

MELCHIOR

With no other extremely pressing matter looming, Addison and I decide to leave the very next day.

The dream was disturbing—and that was before I realized Addison shared it with me. If there is a message in it for us, an actionable one, we need confirmation, as much as I am loath to admit it. I do not like dealing in such nebulous subjects—dreams should be just that: dreams, with no meaning beyond, perhaps, a way to process thoughts and emotions. I do not like that this particular dream has forced me to consider something beyond what I can see and taste and feel, something that is not so easily categorized or proven.

But I am also not going to ignore it just because I am uncomfortable with it. Especially not when it also involved Addison.

I look over at her. The suns shine down on her with their harsh light, her hair shining under it, her cheeks flushed with heat. Moisture coats her skin, causing it to also reflect the light. She continues to trudge forward, her feet sinking with each step she takes. The loss of water through the humans' natural cooling mechanism is quite unfortunate, but they were never built for the climate here on Tajss. Nor were they created to travel across the desert sands with ease.

I take another gliding step, my wings automatically flaring, helping to keep my body light enough that I do not sink despite my greater weight. I have to slow my speed down considerably so I do not leave her behind.

"Are you certain you do not want help?" I ask once again.

Her delicate jaw clenches, and she shakes her head, her eyes focused on the sand in front of her.

"No, I've got this." She glances over at me, her smile somewhat grim. "Thank you."

I nod, resisting the urge to simply grab her and move forward quickly. If she does not want the aid, I do not want to force the issue. Even if it will mean swifter travel. Instead, I focus my energy on the area around us, making certain there are no threats that may catch us unawares. With Addison in my care, I do not want to take any chances.

So as she continues to valiantly fight through the desert she is not physically equipped for, I move forward, my eyes scanning the horizon. Then I circled around to the back and from side to side. Threats could appear from any direction, after all. All the while, I keep a critical eye on Addison. When she appears as though she requires a rest, I stop.

"Why are we stopping?" she asks, wiping at her brow.

"For water and food," I reply easily, moving over to a large rock that casts just enough shade to cover both of us. "Come —we will travel faster if we ensure we take appropriate breaks."

She moves over to me, nodding. Her sigh of relief is heartfelt as the shade covers her and she sits down. Her coloring starts to look better again after some water and dried meat. The rest was necessary.

"How much farther is the Tribe?" she asks, taking another careful sip of water.

"We have traveled perhaps half the distance," I judge, looking out at the desert spread in front of us.

She nods. After a few more minutes of quiet rest, she stands.

"Okay, I'm ready. I know we just stopped because of me," she adds with a slight smile. "Thank you."

I nod. There is no use denying it. We return to our original path and continue to move forward. And I continue to vary my position, scouting all around us while Addison fights through the sand. I hover around her briefly to ensure she does not need another rest. Her coloring is still good and she is continuing to drink water at regular intervals. We can go a bit longer before a break. With a nod, I scout forward once more, my eyes scanning the area automatically.

I am so accustomed to seeing sand and rocks and nothing else at this point that it takes a moment to register that the shapes to the right are not either. The hulking mounds across each creature's back coupled with the sharp spikes scattered over their leathery hide make them easy to identify.

Guster.

Five of them.

The one in front locks its eyes on me, emitting that odd hissing growl, revealing razor-sharp teeth. The group fanned out behind it growls in response. Their speed increases, the wide webbed feet at the end of their thick legs helping them stay above the sand as they move. The shape of their ribs shows through the thick hide, and there is a slight looseness to their skin.

The large lizards are starving—and they have just found a possible meal.

I turn, leap back over the dune that hid them from us and

make my way back to Addison as quickly as possible. There is only time to warn her before they will be upon us.

"A pack of guster are just over that dune," I call out, stopping some distance in front of her. I want to keep some space between her and them. "Move back. Now!" I order.

Her face pales as she stumbles to a halt.

"Guster?" she repeats.

"Yes. Go!"

She nods rapidly, stepping back just as the group crests the dune directly in front of us.

I swing my lochaber, warming my wrists and forearms, and focus on the guster leading the group. The fact that it is larger and positioned in the front tells me that it is the alpha of the pack.

If I kill it, there is a possibility that it will activate the others' flight response, a panic reaction to their leader dying.

Or it could trigger them to attack.

I need to take the chance. There is no other way.

The group rushes at me, but the leader is going faster than the others, a substantial amount of distance between it and the rest.

Good. It will give me more time.

Its eyes lock on mine, the predatory hunger in them clear. When I am certain its attention is fully on me, I deliberately start to move to the side.

Away from Addison and her retreat.

I need to keep their attention fully on me. To that end, I keep spinning the lochaber, hoping the excess movement, the sparkle and shine of the metal in the sun, will help hold their attention.

It works. The alpha veers over to me, its tail flicking behind it in a sinuous motion, its jaws agape.

It charges, putting in the last bit of speed it has left to add.

I hold my ground for a beat. I need to time this well...

When I can almost feel the heat of its breath on me, I leap into the air and slice down at the head, my wings helping me hold the apex of the jump long enough so I can aim. But it whips around faster than I expect it to, the loss of some of its bulk making it more flexible. I shift, pulling my blade out and attempting to dodge the sharp teeth.

I half succeed.

I grunt as the teeth rake my calf, but I yank my leg out quickly enough that it cannot bite down and lock its jaws on me.

I land on the sand, the wounds bleeding sluggishly. They are not too deep.

Enraged at the close call and by the wound I have inflicted, the guster attacks again immediately, its eyes now crazed. Already starving, it has nothing to lose.

"Melchior!" Addison cries out in fear.

I do not turn to look. I know the others are coming towards me, not her.

I run towards the alpha this time, adjusting the grip on the handle of my weapon. I need to ensure this wound is mortal.

Closer.

Closer...

I veer to the right at last moment, stabbing at the thing's eye using all of my force.

It slows me down and locks me into place long enough that it manages to whip its tail around, bending its body almost in half as it crashes into my side.

I grit my teeth at the burst of pain, but I know there was not enough force in the blow to truly damage me, not when it had to bend so far. I keep my grip on the handle, shoving the blade even farther into the wound that was once its eye, my feet skidding in the sand, the muscles in my arms burning at the force required to pierce past the eye.

It screeches, whipping its tail at me again, targeting the same area on my side. I wince at the pain. With a few more hits, it might break my ribs, so I cannot allow it those few more hits.

Not when Addison is not yet safe.

With a roar, I use my fear at that thought to drive the blade in the rest of the way, cracking through the bone of the skull, sliding into the brain just past it.

The guster jerks, its entire body spasming as I cut into its head.

I twist, grunting.

It shudders.

And finally falls limp. The tail falls to the ground, no longer attempting to beat me. The great ribcage stills.

Adjusting my grip on the handle of my lochaber, I pull hard. It releases the blade with a squelching sound. I step back, turning towards the rest of the group, not waiting to watch as the body falls to the ground.

Three of the others have already turned around, running back in the direction they came from.

The fourth is still coming...

I widen my stance, readying myself... But, with only another stride left between us, it hisses at me, and turns sharply to the side, scrambling up the dune to run away as well. I stay tensed, alert, the sound of my breath harsh as I watch them flee.

"Melchior, you're hurt!"

I relax somewhat, finally shifting my attention when Addison hurries over to my side.

"Minor wounds," I reassure her, looking down at cuts in my calf and my reddened side. It will bruise, but when I feel it there is no deeper damage.

"Let me get a look at the cuts at least," she insists, using her water to wet a scrap of fabric she takes out of her pack.

Warmed at her concern, I stay still as she crouches down, frowning while she uses the water and the fabric to clean the gouges. They have already stopped bleeding and are beginning to scab.

Even under the circumstances, I enjoy the softness of her hands, the delicate way in which she touches me. It is so different from how I or the other Zmaj administer to wounds.

Apparently reassured after cleaning the wounds, she stands up again.

"Thank you," she murmurs, meeting my eyes. Hers are serious, sincere. "You saved my life."

"No thanks are needed," I reassure her, looking away to collect myself and to scan the area around us again. I do not like that we have stayed in the same spot for even this long. "Though..." I turn back to her. "I do have a request."

"Anything," she agrees immediately. "What do you need?"

"Can I help you travel the rest of the way? We will shorten our journey. And I want to leave this area as quickly as possible."

In case the guster circle back around to us, decide the danger is worth the hunt with their bellies so empty.

Addison looks around uneasily, understanding my concern.

"Yes," she agrees. "You're right."

I feel a wash of relief. The more quickly we reach the Tribe, the sooner she will be safe.

"Thank you. If you will position yourself here..."

I maneuver her so she is on the side that was not bruised in the attack, wrapping my arm around her slender waist securely. The side of her body presses up against the side of mine in one long line. She hesitates slightly when she wraps her own arm around my waist, so I reach down and tighten it.

"Hold on securely," I warn. "I do not want to worry that you will fall or hurt yourself."

She nods, holding me more tightly, biting her lip as she does so. Her cheeks are pink with embarrassment.

I feel the flush of reaction myself, my entire body tingling from the contact, my entire being focused on her.

"Ready?" I murmur, my voice lower than usual, a reaction to her proximity. I inhale deeply, the scent of her familiar and exciting.

"Yes."

I nod. Flaring my wings, I leap into the air, moving swiftly. I want to travel as quickly as I can. Addison makes a small, surprised sound, her grip tightening on me even more. I skim over the sand, the desert flying past us, my head turning from side to side to ensure we do not run headlong into danger.

The entire time, despite everything, I am acutely aware of her small, slender body pressed up against mine. Of the wild beat of her heart, a flutter I can feel against my torso. Of her soft skin, a slender strip of it revealed by the way her shirt slowly creeps up from my hold. It is just as smooth as I imagined it would be. And her hair...it brushes up against me teasingly with every movement, silky and shining...

The surreptitious glances she sends me and her elevated heartbeat tell me she is not immune to physical closeness.

What would it be like to revel in all that softness? To be able to touch her everywhere, taste her...?

I suppress a growl, the images flooding my mind more than distracting. My cocks harden in response. I attempt to shift my attention to something else, to focus on anything and everything else. But I am only somewhat successful, and only for brief periods. By the time we arrive at the Tribe's cave system, my attention is so fixed on her, I do not know how I can maintain my composure, even in front of the others.

I set down just outside the wall, letting go of Addison even though I want to pull her even closer. She steps away immediately, turning towards me.

"Thank you, Melchior," she murmurs, looking up to meet my eyes. The warmth in her expression, in her dark eyes, draws me in. And it is as though she feels the same connection, the same draw, her eyes not leaving mine as we both simply stare at each other. The trip here was more than simply travel. It managed to bring us closer together, to strengthen this bond that has been building between us. Our attention is so completely fixed on each other that we do not realize anyone else is around us until Bashir calls out a greeting.

I watch Addison start, her face reddening as she turns to return the greeting. I am a bit slower in my own response.

"Welcome," he murmurs, looking between the two of us. His eyes sharpen when he notices the wounds on my calf. "Did you encounter trouble?" he asks, looking beyond us into the desert.

"A pack of starving guster," I explain, forcing my mind back on track.

"A pack?" Bashir repeats, appearing startled.

"Five of them," Addison confirms. "Melchior killed one and the others ran."

"Ah." Bashir turns back to me. "How far?"

"Close enough," I return. "We can go gather the meat now."

We cannot afford to waste the opportunity, not when stores are running low. But I did not want to spend more time there than necessary with Addison, and it would have been difficult to carry a good amount of meat while holding her, in any case.

Bashir nods. "I am ready."

"Go inside, Addison. I will return shortly."

She nods as females begin to trickle out to greet her. She smiles at them and something inside me eases. She will be fine here while we travel back to the guster.

"Let us go," I say.

Bashir returns briefly to his cave to get his small traveling pack and weapons, which all Zmaj have packed and ready to go at a moment's notice. We leave the safety of the Tribe almost as soon as we arrive.

I lead the way back to the guster with Bashir next to me, a little to the side. He asks me some polite questions.

"How was your journey apart from the attack."

"Fine," I return. A beat of silence where I do not expand upon my answer.

"Everything is as it should be in the city?"

"Yes."

When I do not give a more detailed response to that question either, Bashir does not ask any more. My uneasiness around him elicits the same response from him. He senses that I am avoiding something. But I cannot help myself. So I simply focus on the task at hand, which is the best I can do.

Luckily, without Addison's added weight, the trip back to the guster is even swifter. I can see Bashir is on high alert when we stop next to the beast, just as I am. But there is no sign the other guster have been back here or that they are anywhere in the immediate area anymore.

"I will take the head. You take the tail," Bashir murmurs.

I nod. With that small bit of necessary communication out of the way, we both draw our long hunting knives and get to work on the thick hide. There is not as much meat on this guster as there would be on one that was well fed, but even this amount is valuable. The guster eat epis, their meat infused with the plant. It makes them even more nourishing than other game.

After skinning the animal, we make quick work of cutting out the meat, placing the pieces in our packs to take back to the Tribe. It does not take long at all, not with Bashir and me to do the butchering together. We have much experience, our knives slicing and cutting almost intuitively. I focus fully on the task at hand. I know I am avoiding the issue, avoiding the very reason we traveled here in the first place, but I need some time before I can speak of the matter.

So I wait.

I wait until we pack the meat and travel back to the Tribe, until I find Addison again, who is clearly waiting for our return. When I know it is time, when I know I cannot delay the discussion any longer, I still hesitate. I scoffed when Bashir had spoken of Tajss as an entity in and of itself, when he'd spread around to everyone the fact that children were having dreams.

I scoffed.

I thought he was foolish to put so much stock into emotions and dreams, to perpetuate anything that he did not have proof of. I thought what he was doing was simply dangerous, something that appeared to be laying down the groundwork for worship of a higher power, for religion that could easily be used to harm.

But now... I feel as though my world has been turned upon its head. Not only do I have to accept the matter, I must swallow my pride, rise above what the human females call "ego," and give Bashir a chance to make sense of the seemingly telepathic dream Addison and I shared. I would be lying if I did not admit, at least to myself, that my desire to be near Addison outside work situations partly fuels the decision.

The situation is baffling, but considering Maeve and

Padraig and their growing telepathic connection... It is almost as if they have become one unit rather than two, each making up a complimentary portion of their bonded whole. They have yet to take part in a mating ceremony, but that is simply because of the current troubles plaguing us. Their bond grows ever stronger.

I take a deep breath and approach Bashir.

"Bashir...may we please speak with you? In private?"

Bashir turns from where he set down the meat in the kitchen, his expression curious.

"Yes, of course," he agrees immediately, making me feel even more ashamed for my distant manner. "Follow me to my cave."

I agree. We walk after him as he leads the way. Perhaps my feet drag somewhat, but I have accepted the inevitable. When we reach his unit, Bashir gestures for us to take a seat. We do so, and he follows suit, his gaze fixed on my face.

"Now...why have you been attempting to avoid conversing with me?" he asks, not bothering to avoid the tension between us.

I shake my head, clasping my hands.

"I have been...reluctant," I admit. "It is...a difficult subject for me."

"I see," he murmurs. "You may begin as you wish."

I nod, attempting to organize my thoughts rather than simply allowing them to spew forth.

"I... dreamed." Bashir's eyes sharpen, and he leans forward. But he doesn't speak, simply listens intently. "It was an unusual dream. One of Tajss, of the wonder to be found here...but then it shifted. And the wonder gave way to desolation, a sense of... danger. And... Addison was in the dream."

He nods once more, his expression thoughtful.

"And Addison shared the dream," Bashir murmurs. It is not a question.

"How did you know?" Addison demands, frowning.

He smiles slightly. "A dream only Melchior had would not be enough to bring him here to my doorstep, let alone with you by his side," he explains. "Now—I need a more detailed description of what you saw. Were they images? Projected emotions? In what manner did you see Addison?"

The dam now broken, the information spills out of me. I tell him of the images, the animals, the landscape. And of Addison. How I saw her.

She interjects with details from her dream as well, of how she saw me. And how the dream ended with both of us holding hands, our expressions pleading. Something vast looking out at us from behind our own faces...

When the words finally slow, then stop, Bashir continues to sit silently, a slight frown between his brows.

"Hmm." He shakes his head, clasping his hands in front of him. "The babies have had more dreams, but the messages are not yet clear..."

I wait, feeling disappointment rise inside myself.

How can I trust a system that cannot give me a real, unequivocal answer? What is the point of any answer if it is based on this mystical, shaky premise, this unstable ground? I do not see how it could help us. So far, all these dreams and visions have done is distract us—not good when we are under the threat of attack.

Bashir meets my eyes as the thoughts pass through my mind. His eyes are direct, calm, penetrating. I look away, struck by the notion that Bashir can sense my disbelief. But he does not remark upon it when he speaks.

"You both have a role to play." I turn my head to meet his eyes once more. "A role that will reveal itself over time." He shifts his eyes over to Addison. "Like Maeve, Padraig, and the babies, you have been chosen for something. Make no mistake."

Bashir's look is confident, a look I know well.

My dragon brother is very self-assured when it comes to his beliefs—to the point of knowing.

"But chosen for what?" Addison asks. It is the question I have as well, though I have not asked because I know what the answer will be.

"I do not know," Bashir replies readily, open at least in that aspect. "But I am confident the pieces will come together."

Addison and I look at each other. It is not an answer, at least not one we can do anything with.

Wait and see. That is all Bashir says we can do.

Penelope enters then, hands laden with plates of food.

"I think it's time to take a break from serious talk and have some food," she announces, setting them down on the table nearby. "Addison and Melchior have traveled all the way from the city—I'm certain they're both hungry and tired."

"Thanks, Penelope," Addison murmurs, smiling.

"Thank you," I add as well, standing to follow the others over to the table.

Bashir pulls Penelope into a warm hug, kissing her soundly. He whispers something into her ear and her smile widens as a blush warms her cheeks. She pushes him away, shaking her head, but her eyes are shining with happiness. As are his when he comes to sit down with us.

I sit down as well, watching out of the corner of my eye as she returns with the rest of the food, taking a seat next to Bashir at the table. He reaches out to take her hand before he even takes a bite of the food.

I cannot help the fantasy that forms in my mind at the entire interaction. Cannot help but dream of the potential future between Allison and me that looks just like this.

Penelope murmurs something and Bashir chuckles,

raising her hand to his lips before offering her a morsel of food.

I feel a pang in my heart. Domestic, settled, and... home. It warms my heart to see it even while I feel myself tense.

I dare not look at Addison, for fear she will see the hope shining in my eyes. Does she feel my interest? Does she feel the same?

Or am I pining for a future such as this alone?

7

ADDISON

*W*e decide to sleep in Tribe territory and leave early in the morning. I'm totally fine with that, happy to see the others, and delay the long, harsh trip back to the city while I can.

I sigh, turning over on the pallet. I don't know what I expected when I came here, but I do know I thought I would leave with some answers. Instead, I feel like I only have more questions.

I could see the frustration in Melchior's eyes as he realized that as well and could completely understand the sentiment. I felt the same way.

But I also know Bashir was simply being honest. The truth is, none of us has any answers yet, not really. We're all just trying to muddle along, hoping we're doing what we're supposed to. Maybe I could talk to Maeve...

My thoughts come in a steady stream, one after another, until I exhaust myself. At last, I finally fall into a deep sleep.

At least...I think so?

Am I dreaming?

It doesn't feel quite right...

The vastness of Tajss greets me.

I am treated to a bird's-eye view of the rolling sand dunes, the craggy rocks, the color leached out into gray tones under the night sky.

A familiar group of guster run underneath me, and I know with the surety of dreams that they are the same ones we encountered the day before. I don't feel alarmed at the sight of them. They're far away, moving in farther. I do not know how I know, but I do.

I soar past them.

Past a small oasis with a crystal-clear pool in the center, the starlight reflecting from its surface.

Past another rock formation.

And then the dream accelerates somehow. The land below starts to whip past, blurring slightly. The light begins to change, the weak glow of the just-rising suns beginning to touch the high points of the terrain below.

Abruptly, I slow down again, wherever I am, floating above Tajss. There's movement below.

I frown, even in the dream. What is that? There are so many of them, maybe an insect of some kind.

As if the dream is sensing my confusion, I'm abruptly closer to the ground below, close enough that I can now make out more details. They aren't insects. I feel a chill flow through me as I recognize the textured blue skin, the elongated heads.

One of them throws its head back and lets out that distinctive staccato yell, revealing the full black eyes, the lipless slit of its mouth, parting to display sharp teeth and tusks curving out front.

Alien invaders—a whole lot of them.

I feel my anxiety rising as I continue to pass over them. It takes too long to reach the edge of the crowd. There are too many of them. Finally, there's sand below, but I don't relax, because directly ahead is a very familiar structure.

A wall.

Panic hits me, hard and fast.

I need to wake up!

Wake up, Addison!

Wake up!

My eyes slam open and I bolt upright.

"Melchior!"

His name isn't even fully out of my mouth before he's there in the doorway of the small cave I'm staying in, his face grim.

"Did you see—" My voice comes out shrill, panicky, though I don't want it to.

"The invaders," he finishes grimly. "Yes. They're headed this way."

Another chill goes through me, even as I register a lack of surprise. The dream was so real I didn't even question that it could be anything but a warning. But it wasn't a dream, was it?

I don't know if I fell asleep at all.

A chill floods me.

A vision.

It was a vision, and it doesn't shock me at all that Melchior saw it, not after the visceral recognition in the vision that what I was seeing was actually happening.

I immediately jump to my feet. By mutual accord, we rush outside. Melchior takes a deep breath and lets out a roar that I feel in my stomach, it's so loud.

"Attack!"

For sure, everyone in the whole cave system heard that. Within fifteen seconds, people start spilling out, weapons in hand. Lochabers for the Zmaj, and the sharpened poles that the women have come up with for defense.

I slow as we near the wall. Now that we're outside, the sound of footsteps just past it is audible. A lot of footsteps.

I see the Zmaj running for gate that leads outside. Right beyond it, I can just make out the invaders closing in. It was one thing to see them from high up in a dream. Another altogether to see the mass of them coming directly at us, a wall of matte brown carapace armor, teeming with arms and pincers, the staccato sounds of so many together blending until it sounds like a dull roar. The shock of seeing it like this brings me to a halt as I stare.

"Stay behind the wall," Melchior orders, looking into my eyes, only once, then continuing forward with his lochaber.

I nod, still staring. How are we going to defend against that?

I turn to see Zmaj and other women still rushing out, ready to defend the stronghold. They're in place with time to spare. The shared vision Melchior and I had ensured at least that much of an edge.

I step forward, but then stop. Melchior can be of actual, valuable help out there on the front lines, but my talents lie elsewhere. I turn away from the place everyone else is rushing to, and head over to the machine responsible for the shields.

We know there's a problem with the glass holding charge, with the longevity of the shields. I need to be on hand to do what I can. I reach the machine just as I hear the invaders engage with the Zmaj. I wince as I hear the crunch of bone, the cries of pain. Some things are universal, aren't they?

The machine is set higher up, high enough that I can see past the wall.

The Zmaj deliberately formed a line just at the shield's edge, ready and waiting for the invaders to funnel through the small opening, the only space they could get through. It's a highly defensible position, with the wall as a second line of defense. Of course, if they don't defend that opening and masses flood through, the wall will only be a delaying mechanism. Ensuring they have to funnel through will allow our forces to pick them off as they come in.

A familiar flash of bronze scales draws my eyes.

Melchior.

I watch as he takes a position in the front lines, his lochaber held confidently in front of him, his stance alert. I feel a stab of fear as the invaders finally reach the shields.

There are so many of them, they almost behave like a liquid, hitting the shield and pooling, their numbers widening around it, testing the boundaries, even as they inevitably start to funnel through the small, deliberate opening.

From my vantage point, I can see just how much of a difference there is in our numbers. There are a lot of them. Too many.

I look back at Melchior, watching anxiously as he easily disposes of one of the creatures, smashing it in the face with the handle end of his weapon.

He dodges the next one as it slices at him with a short sword, the lethal blade just missing his side.

I hiss at that near call.

Whirling around, he brings the lochaber down in an odd looping motion the invader cannot defend against. Its head rolls off and onto the ground in the next instant, but there are ever more of the creatures rushing in to take its place.

The knot in my gut is nearly unbearable, even though I know he has to be brave. Even though I know I shouldn't be feeling so protective of him. It isn't like we're together, not like we're in a relationship even if we apparently share dreams and visions now. We're just friends. Co-workers even.

Then the shields flicker. It's barely noticeable, there and gone, but it sure catches my attention.

And the attention of the invaders pressed up right against the curve.

A couple of them pop through at the flicker, clearly shocked at how abruptly they've left their friends behind on the other side of the shield. Two of the Zmaj break off and make quick work of them, but if the shields fall—we'll be overrun in no time.

Shit.

Shit shit shit.

I glare down at the machine.

My original idea was to replace the glass, but that will mean a downtime of maybe fifteen seconds, if all goes well. That's fifteen seconds too many with that freaking army pressed up against the shield, just waiting for an opportunity.

"Think, Addison," I mutter, staring at the machine. I go through and discard various ideas, my brain hyper-focused. Melchior is down there, at ground zero. I need a solution. Now.

"Okay, okay, okay," I mutter to myself, standing to pace. "If I can't replace the glass, I need to replace the charge. But I can't take the fucking glass out..." I freeze.

There was a spare part Kate left behind...

It just might work. I run back through the cave system, hoping the part is still where I remember it being . . . that it's the one I think it is . . . that it'll actually work.

I almost sob with relief when I find it.

Picking it up with a grunt, I run back the way I came, the other women giving me curious glances as they stand ready to defend their home if any of the invaders manage to get through.

"What are you doing, Addison?" Fallon calls out as I pass her.

"Trying to get the shields to hold!" I yell back, my arms burning from the weight of the part. I reach the shield generator, falling down to my knees with the part. I'm definitely going to feel those bruises later, but I ignore the pain.

The shield flickers again, this time for longer. I look out there, see a sudden influx of maybe twenty more of the invaders. A couple of them get through the Zmaj this time, the group too large to keep back. The women step up with their sharpened poles, stabbing and skewering the would-be slavers. I look away grimly.

The next flicker might be even longer.

And that will be that.

But I have to shut out that thought as my hands move swiftly, steady and accurate. I can't mess up.

This, right here in front of me, this is all that can matter to me right now.

Taking a deep breath, I connect the thing, cutting and twisting some wires together, making sure I don't jostle the glass and break it while I struggle to get the new addition into place. It's just a hair too large to fit comfortably, so I have to wiggle it just right, aware of the fragile nature of some of the parts...

Click.

There!

Okay, now if I just slide this over, it should produce an energy loop that should keep the shield at full capacity for hours.

Not forever—if I keep it connected the way it is, the glass will explode with the constant rush of input. It will need to be disconnected periodically to keep that from happening— but that's a problem for the future. We can install alternate shields when that downtime needs to happen with the main system. And that can wait until we're not under fucking attack, right? Right.

I slide the final part into place and hold my breath. If I did it wrong, the shields might fail altogether.

I stare at the translucent energy field, fear a cold, hard rock in my stomach.

It doesn't fail.

In fact, the thing brightens. It looks stronger.

Excitement rises up inside me as I get to my feet, looking down at the melee at the front.

They have things back under control, the invaders funneling neatly through the only place they can. My eyes find Melchior, still fighting, obviously healthy and whole, his lochaber swinging forcefully.

I... did it.

I mean, we're not out of the woods yet, but if the shields stay strong and we continue to mow through the attacking army like this, we will survive.

I almost can't believe it. I look at the shield generator again.

"You ugly piece of twisted metal," I murmur in awe. "Thank God you're here." I don't give a rat's ass about how it looks if it works!

I stay in place for a bit longer to make sure the shield continues to hold.

Then I run down to grab a pointed spear of my own and join the women inside, ready to defend against the invading horde. With the shield now in place and the funnel intact, it turns out to be more of a wait just in case scenario.

Something I'm totally for as I watch the Zmaj mow down creature after creature, their muscular bodies flexing and leaping tirelessly, lochabers swinging hard as they chop and stab at the attackers.

I start to wonder if the mob is never-ending, if there will always be more of those armored bodies, more of those blue-skinned faces behind any that are taken down. But eventually, the rush turns into more of a trickle. And then the trickle turns to stragglers. And then the onslaught is over.

I almost don't believe it as the quiet settles over us, the sounds of lochabers, of swords and knives, of cries of battle and of death finally gone. The quiet feels almost too quiet after hearing it for so long. We all wait, as if to make sure it really is the end.

When no more of the invaders show up, sentries are posted to keep an eye out, and the Zmaj finally come back inside, exhaustion clear on each and every face.

But spirits are also high. By some miracle, despite the length of the battle, there were no casualties. There are some wounds that need to be tended to immediately, but mostly everyone got away with only minor ones.

My eyes automatically search for Melchior—there! Covered in gore and sweaty from battle, he looks tired but otherwise whole as he comes in with the rest. His head swivels from side to side too, until his eyes land on me and linger. I wait in place as he walks over.

"Are you all right?" I ask when he stops directly in front of me.

"Yes. And you?" he scans me, even though I've been on this side of both the shields and the wall this whole time.

"Better than you," I point out.

He smiles tiredly.

"Yes." He glances back at the carnage that will have to be taken care of at some point. Just not immediately. "I saw you go to the shield generator." He turns back around, his gaze thoughtful. "How did you stop the shields from failing?"

"I made an energy loop with a spare part Kate left behind. But it isn't a permanent fix," I warn. "If we leave it as is for too long, the glass will explode."

He shakes his head, the admiration in his eyes warming me from the inside out.

"You are the reason we all survived today," he says. "And if the glass explodes now, we will simply sweep it up and thank it for lasting."

That surprises a grin from me. "True."

"Guys! Who wants breakfast?" Fallon's voice has both of us looking over.

The women are already heading over to the kitchen, getting the cooking going.

"We should wait here until the afternoon," Melchior murmurs. "To be sure there is not going to be another attack."

I nod. That makes sense. Melchior needs rest. We could be helpful here, plus it's probably safer for us to leave when the suns are fully up in the sky, and we can see threats coming from farther away.

So we stay.

I head over to help with the food prep while the Zmaj go to clean up after the fight.

The division of labor feels a little old-school, but it's also just plain practical under the circumstances. With so many hands on deck, it doesn't take long to get the food together.

"How did the two of you...know?" Penelope asks as we all sit down to eat. "That we were about to be attacked, I mean?"

"Yeah, how did you know?" Fallon reiterates, frowning. "The sentries and scouts still hadn't sent a warning over. You were way ahead of them."

I take a deep breath and let it out, a little uncomfortable with saying this out loud, but it's what happened. I've never tried to run from the truth. Well. Usually.

"We both had a dream...a vision," I explain. "We...saw the invaders coming towards us. Towards the wall."

"A vision?" Olivia repeats, exchanging a glance with Mei. "How did you..."

Mei leans towards me.

"How did you know it was real?" she finishes for Olivia. It's a fair question.

"We both had the same one at the same time."

That sets all of them back in their seats. I can see them trying to process it. That's all right. I'm still not sure I have. I take another bite of food.

"That's...amazing," Bailey finally murmurs. "I'm so glad you were here!"

That gets a round of agreement from the others.

And sets off a round of questions in me. Was that the reason for that first dream we shared? I frown down at my plate. Was it simply to get us out here to the Tribe in time? Did Tajss accurately predict what our response to sharing that dream would be?

Were we maneuvered?

As the talk moves on to other matters, like the cleanup that's going to be necessary outside and then the shielding, I come back to the conversation. Whether my suspicions are true or not, I'm glad we were here to circumvent what could have been a real catastrophe.

"The workaround I did to keep the shields up isn't a solution that can just be left as-is. We need to put a backup in place to cover so the glass can be changed out before it explodes from the pressure. Without being left without a shield to speak of in the interim."

"Shit, we'll take it," Fallon mutters, looking around at the others. "Those shields saved our butts today, Addison."

The murmurs of agreement are all heartfelt. I feel a little uncomfortable at the attention, but luckily, the children break up the moment.

Zoe runs up to Olivia, trailing the twins who run up to their own mother, Mei. They're all ridiculously adorable, with their rounded faces and tiny horns.

"Mom, look what I found!" Zoe cries out, holding up a pretty rock.

"Me too!" both Elneese and Ganeese chime in, holding up their own loot.

Everyone laughs as the kids run around the table to show off the glimmering rocks.

When Zoe runs up to me, her blue eyes shining, her pretty red hair up in two lopsided ponytails, I feel my heart swell.

When she trips as she gets to me, I move fast, wrapping an arm around her tiny waist.

"Whoah, there! Are you okay?"

She nods at me, her eyes large as she holds out the rock.

"Oh, wow!" I exclaim dutifully, bending over to get a good look. "That is truly gorgeous."

"Gorgeous," she repeats, her little rosebud mouth curving as she repeats the word. "Mom, it's gorgeous!" she announces, running away once more.

I chuckle, paying Elneese and Ganeese the same attention so they don't feel left out. All the while, I feel almost an ache as I watch all the beautiful children, a combination of both their Zmaj fathers and their human mothers. Like they're awakening a maternal instinct inside me. I feel a flash of unease at the thought, so I push it away. I have no desire to be like my mom. I try to keep that part of me locked down as we finish breakfast. It's safer that way.

We don't spend much more time with the Tribe in any case. By the time afternoon rolls around, we're back out in the desert.

This time, Melchior helps me across. After seeing exactly how much faster and easier it is to travel with his help, it seems silly to refuse to do so. Especially if it means we're ultimately safer because we're spending less time on the journey. It doesn't mean that I'm not fully and completely aware of his body, his closeness, the feel of his arm around me...

I glance up at his face, highlighted by the blazing suns. His gaze is intent, focused on the space around us, watching for any threats. I look away again, the feminine part of me responding in a way I wouldn't have expected. Yeah, I can take care of myself. But it's nice knowing Melchior is there too, especially out here.

Because I'm attached to Melchior like a monkey, we reach the city a whole lot faster than I would have expected. Unfortunately, my expectation of getting back into the swing of things, settling back into my routine, is immediately dashed.

As soon as we enter, we see Zmaj warriors gathering, a sense of urgency in the air. Melchior's jaw clenches at the sight, his eyes scanning the crowd.

"There," he says abruptly. "Visidion."

I hurry after him as he makes his way through the crowd. What is going on?

Visidion turns to Melchior when we near, his face hard.

"The mining settlement is under siege," he announces before either of us can ask what's going on. "Can you come?"

Melchior doesn't even hesitate. "Yes."

What? I feel completely flummoxed at this sudden turn of events. The mining settlement is under siege? And Melchior's going to run off into that danger? I feel my heart racing too fast in my chest, feel a slight edge of nausea at the thought.

Forcing myself to take a deep breath, I try to think passed the triggered emotions. Melchior isn't my father. I'm not a little girl again, watching her dad leave her. But damned if I'll just stand back and allow shit to happen.

I'm an adult now. I have the power to decide what I'm going to do. And I refuse to let him leave alone.

"I'm coming too," I announce, feeling the rightness of that

decision in my bones. This is the first time I'll be signing up to join relief efforts, and I know it's the right decision.

Melchior turns to me in surprise, scowling.

"What?" he asks, reaching out to grip my arm, pulling me to the side. "It is not safe, Addison! You cannot come!"

"You're still going," I point out stubbornly. "I'm coming. Unless you'll stay?" He shakes his head, frowning. "Yeah, I thought so."

"I want you to remain here. Where it is safe," he tries, his tone softening.

I shake my head in return. "No, I'm coming." I slide my hand over his, where it still grips my arm. His hold is firm but gentle. He would never hurt me, not intentionally. "Who else can you have visions with? Who else can watch out for you?" I ask, meeting his concerned gaze. I understand the concern.

I don't want him to go either, but I know trying to keep him here isn't a good idea. I don't think he would listen anyway, his sense of responsibility is too great. It's one of the reasons why I admire him so much. He's just a good person, deep down, where it counts.

His face softens at my question, his hand loosening somewhat.

"There is that," he agrees, his eyes searching my face. "I simply...want you safe."

I swallow past the knot that appears in my throat. I can see that. Can see that he wants me to be safe. And I understand.

I don't know what this is between us, if it's going to just be friendship or if we're going to move into something more, but in either case, I care too much about him not to want to keep him completely safe too. But we don't live in a world where we can do that. There's danger around every corner and sometimes we have to face it head on.

"Melchior...there's no place that's completely safe here on Tajss," I murmur.

He sighs, his eyes shifting from mine to my hand where it still rests against his. He's quiet for a moment, a mix of emotions crossing his face. But eventually he relents. Like he's having a hard time telling me "no." When his eyes meet mine once more, there's acceptance in them.

"You will not take unnecessary risks," he orders.

"Of course not," I agree. "I'm not Rambo."

He frowns. "Rambo?"

"I'm not an idiot," I try instead. "I'll be safe." As safe as the situation allows anyway.

He nods, the anxiety still touching his face while everyone rushes around us. But there's no way to completely alleviate his fears, not when we're headed directly for the danger.

You know, I used to be bored on the ship sometimes.

Sometimes...I really miss that.

8

MELCHIOR

*W*e still have some time before we leave for the mining settlement. Addison and I are going with Kate and Errol in the rover, but we have to wait for them to arrive. I decide to use the time in a productive manner.

"Wait, Addison. Hold it angled, like this..."

I adjust the shock stick, fixing her hold on it at the same time. If she does not master the hold, it will be knocked out of her hand before she can do any damage.

"I do not know if this is the best idea," Errol warns from where he is watching on the sidelines. "The stick needs more work before I would be comfortable relying on it as a weapon in a true battle situation."

"It is what we have. And it could possibly help even the odds in a fight," I return, stepping back. "I want her to at least know how to use it properly. And if the shocking aspect of it fails, at least it can still be used to bludgeon."

The long, club-like weapon has two metal prongs at the end of it. With meteorite glass inserted into the compartment in the middle, the energy from it can be channeled in such a way as to create a shock at the end. Strong enough to stun a human-sized creature and at the very least cause pain for anything we might encounter. I know it is not perfect, but I want to use everything we have at our disposal to ensure Addison's safety.

She was right when she pointed out that nowhere is really safe on Tajss currently. After she made that point, even the logical side of my brain had to acquiesce to her argument. Not just the emotional part of me, the part that wanted to give her anything and everything she desired.

In light of the fact that the attacks on our settlements are now clearly being coordinated, I do not want to leave her behind, leave her vulnerable here without me to protect her.

It is plain the invaders are looking for every angle they can exploit. Attacking multiple targets at once would fall in line with that.

That does not mean that I do not still have misgivings about bringing her along for relief efforts. I certainly will not be allowing her use the shock stick and engage in any kind of hand-to-hand combat unless it is strictly necessary, unless there is simply no other choice. And I do not think it will come to that. There are enough dragons going to the mining settlement together that I firmly believe the situation should be contained relatively quickly.

"Then I shall leave you to your endeavors."

Errol nods at Addison, taking a step back. He has said his piece and decided to stop intervening while we practice, which I appreciate.

Addison watches him leave, her face concerned, pensive. When she turns back to me, I force my own face into optimistic lines, attempting to bring my mood up to match. She's been watching me intently and I do not want to frighten her. She displays a brave front at most times, but I am no fool. I know sometimes the outside only masks the true feelings within.

"Once more, Addison," I say, keeping my voice relaxed. "Make sure you do not leave yourself vulnerable when you strike." We start to circle once more. With the basics of holding such a weapon already taught, along with basic strikes and defense, I want to give her a taste of what a true fight would be like. Nobody will stand still to wait for her to hurt them. "You must be strategic, attack when you have the best possibility of success."

She nods, her gaze focused on me. Scanning. Watching. In a normal scenario, she would have absolutely no chance of defeating a Zmaj warrior. We are simply too well-trained, our reach and strength too much greater than a human's, female or male. Perhaps if she were lucky, caught one of us by surprise with a weapon such as this, she might have a chance.

However, she will not be facing the Zmaj. She will not be facing anyone in a fight if all goes as planned, but if it does not, her opponents will be the invaders. And they do not have the same reach, strength, or the ability to leap as high, wingless as they are.

And Addison is not a completely helpless female. After the human females created the sharpened poles to help them fight, they have been practicing with them, so Addison's footwork is not that of a complete novice.

I watch her, deliberately stumbling slightly as I move, giving her an opening... She lunges into my guard quickly, tapping at my chest with the shock stick.

"Excellent," I praise.

She smiles in response, her face aglow. "I know you let me do it, but I don't care!" she admits. "That was still great! Woohoo!" She thrusts her hands up in the air in victory.

I chuckle, happy to see her happy. "Let us continue then," I urge. "The more practice we are able to have before we must leave, the better it will be for you."

She nods, focusing once more. "Okay. I'm ready."

I mock attack her from different angles, going slower than I can so she can learn. When she leaves her middle vulnerable, I tap it.

"Do not take the attack if you will sacrifice your defense. Being mortally wounded defeats the purpose."

She nods, adopting a more serious expression as she steps back. While I continue to work with her, I realize something else. I am... having fun. Not what I expected, but I am enjoying her company, enjoying her enthusiasm, her focus. The physical closeness. Though that cuts both ways.

I attempt to remain sharp, to keep my mind on the task at hand, to touch her in a distant manner, only as a teacher would touch his student. But it is difficult. My hand wants to linger. I have the urge to be closer than I need to. My gaze lingers on her lips, the soft column of her throat, the sway of her breasts under her loose shirt when she moves quickly, the points of her nipples visible underneath, the shape of her backside when she lunges and her clothing tightens. It is taut and round, a perfect handful. I suppress a growl as I adjust her stance once more.

"If you do not keep your feet braced properly, a gentle touch can topple you. And no opponent will use a gentle touch."

She nods, her cheeks flushed, a slight sheen of moisture on her skin. I want to lick it off. I take a deep breath, but it does not help. I only succeed in taking her distinctive scent into my lungs.

I suppress a groan. This is torture indeed. Why did I think this was a good idea?

I am so distracted by the arousal coursing through my body that I accidentally react automatically when she attacks next, sweeping her feet out from under her. Realizing my mistake immediately, I reach out and grab her at the same time, turning so I fall to the ground with her on top of me, cushioning her fall.

"My apologies," I gasp immediately, worried that I was too rough. "Are you hurt?"

She shakes her head, out of breath. "No. I'm okay. Really."

And that is when I realize her entire body is pressed up against mine. The softness of her breasts, her belly, her legs tangled with mine. My hands clench on the curve of her hips, where my hands automatically settled of their own accord.

She watches me with wide eyes as the realization hits her as well, her cheeks, already flushed from exertion, turning even pinker. My eyes fall to her lips. Pink and plump, slightly parted...I want to kiss her, the urge nearly uncontrollable with her on top of me. With her mouth so close...I begin to raise my head...but then Addison turns hers abruptly. I quickly drop mine once more.

"Thank you for helping me learn how to defend myself, Melchior." She turns back to me, her face more composed now. "You're such a good friend."

I feel the blow in my chest, a sharp, clean stab. There and gone. It leaves a dull throbbing behind. I mask the pain she just inflicted with words that appear only sweet on the surface. I answer with the truth.

"I will always be here for you, Addison." I meet her eyes, hoping she can see that I mean every word I say. "Always."

Her eyes linger on mine for a moment...but then she simply nods, rolling off me to reach for the shock stick where it dropped during the fall.

"Thank you, Melchior," she murmurs, holding it with both hands. "I... appreciate that."

I nod myself, reaching my feet more slowly.

"Of course." I clear my throat. After what just happened, I

am reconsidering how we should move forward with the brief training. Sparring suddenly feels too dangerous. At least for right now, directly after the moment we just shared. "I think it best you repeat the movements now, the strikes and the blocks I demonstrated in the beginning."

She nods, her gaze turning inward as she adjusts her stance to stand with her feet shoulder width apart.

"Okay."

Then she begins, moving from one strike to the next, one block to another. She is a good student. She listens to everything I say. I reach out with my fingertips to redirect her when needed, adjusting her hold for different moves, tapping at her calves when her footwork is not exact.

I'm sure to keep my distance, only touching her as much as is necessary, and only from a good length away. But even as I maintain that careful amount of space between us, my skin remains fevered, so aware of her closeness that it almost tingles with it.

However, despite the uncomfortable heat pulsing within me, I cannot help but grin while I watch her. I find myself impressed by exactly how much she has learned in so little time. I continue to correct her here and there, but the corrections are more and more minor.

"Good?" she asks, slightly out of breath from the particularly difficult move she has repeated multiple times.

"Very good. I am impressed at your progress." The praise is honest.

She grins, a touch of shyness to her expression and a vulnerability in her eye that tugs at me. Like everything else about her.

"Really?"

"Yes. Really."

Her smile widens, her cheeks flushing deeper with pleasure. Then I see her eyes drop to my lips. And her cheeks redden even more. The answering heat in me roars to the surface, stronger than ever. Never very far in her presence.

There is something between us. It is more than just my own attraction for her. That tension, that pulse of...something...

I take a step towards her without thinking about it, responding to her. And she does not move back, her eyes rising to meet my own. I can see the answering attraction in them, the answering heat.

I want to kiss her. Want to taste her, touch her... I take another step towards her, close enough now to wrap my arms around her. I start to lift my arms, start to make that irrevocable movement...

Just as someone bursts into the room with a message from Errol.

"The rover is back and ready to go!"

My hands clench at my sides even as I turn to acknowledge the messenger, frustration a bitter taste in my mouth after the sweet anticipation of just a moment earlier. I look over at Addison to see her attention is now on the ground in front of her.

Whatever this is between us...There is no time to explore it. Not now.

For the first time that I can recall, I feel true resentment for my responsibilities.

9

ADDISON

*E*rrol makes a sharp turn.

"Hold on!" he calls out.

I tense, trying my best to maintain my position next to Melchior rather than ending on top of him, but I can't quite manage it.

"Sorry," I mutter as my body presses into his side, the hard muscle of his arm pushing against me.

"It is no problem," he returns in that deep voice.

I straighten as soon as I am able to, my heart beating faster, my face most assuredly flushed. Damn it. I have to sit closer to Melchior in the rover than I'm currently comfortable with. I glance at him from the corner of my eye, taking in his handsome profile, his strong jaw, the thick column of his neck. My eyes drop down to his big hands, corded with strength and sporting faint scars.

I bite my lip, looking away again. Everything about him is just so masculine. It makes me feel so damn feminine, in a way I didn't even realize would affect me so much. I want all that maleness, all that strength, on top of me, wrapped around me.

I shift in my seat at the thought, one that I've been having more and more frequently, if I'm honest. All this enforced closeness is wearing on the little restraint I have around him. I just don't trust myself when it comes to Melchior. We got in the stupid rover while I was already hot and bothered from the training session, and you know what? Spending time pressed up against him like this really hasn't helped me calm down. What a shocker.

The heat from Tajss' blazing suns isn't helping much either. Predictably, I find myself looking over at Melchior again. At the luxurious mane of dark hair. At the small horns he sports. At the curve of his wings. The glitter of his bronze scales, the sunlight doing him all the favors in the world.

And his lips. My eyes zero in on that mouth, with the slightly bigger bottom lip...shit.

I jerk my attention forward once more, almost glaring at Errol in the driver's seat. His peacock blue-green scales glow brightly in the sunlight as well, matching his blue-green eyes. I feel exactly nothing when I stare at his handsome face. Which is good considering he's Kate's mate, the woman who's the only reason our group got out from under that tyrant Annabelle's thumb. But also annoying because it confirms I really don't have eyes for anyone else. If this attraction was just because of looks, someone else should have been able to catch my eye too. But nobody pulls my gaze like Melchior.

I shift my eyes away from Errol, who's all business in the driver's seat, to Kate riding shotgun next to him. Her shock stick is sitting directly in front of her.

"Do you think the shock sticks will help, Kate?" I ask, really just trying to get my mind off of Melchior next to me.

She shrugs, turning in her seat to look at me. As a natural redhead, her skin is even paler than mine, meaning the flush of heat is even more apparent on her. I don't envy her that extra sensitivity to the sun either, not with the suns here. She wipes at her sweaty face with a grimace.

"I figure it's worth training with it even if it's only useful enough to fend off beasts and invaders long enough to run for cover. If it helps us live another day..." She trails off, shrugging again.

"True." We've been too vulnerable for too long here on Tajss.

The truth is, a lot of us are willing to grasp at anything that will help us better defend ourselves, grant us some more independence. I know I was never used to being as dependent on men as I am here. It was something that took a good amount of adjusting to.

Of course, not all the women are on board with trying to become quite so independent, which I understand. The Zmaj keep us insulated from a lot of the danger here.

Heading out with the sharpened poles or shock sticks isn't safe. There is risk involved, a reality all of us understand. I don't blame the ones who aren't fully on board with things like the shock stick. I know, for myself, I'm all for anything that makes me feel more in charge. More in control of my own safety, my own life.

Errol drives the rover over a rocky patch, jostling all of us inside. I bump into Melchior again, and his hand comes out to steady me, gripping my thigh firmly. He lets go as soon as we're back on smooth ground, but the damage is already done. I want to cry out with sexual frustration at that point. I'm only a woman! How am I supposed to take this sustained torture?

Ugh!

From then on, I spend much of the ride skating that edge of sexual frustration. Every time I come down even a little, I get thrown into Melchior again. I grip the seat underneath myself and grit my teeth, trying to focus on the positive and only partially succeeding. At least we haven't encountered any of the many dangerous beasts Tajss has to offer, which is great.

Unfortunately, as soon as I try to focus on that positive, we're derailed by another natural phenomenon. Teach me to be optimistic.

The first clue something is wrong is when Errol jerks the wheel to the side so abruptly even Kate cries out in the front.

"Shit!" she yells, bracing herself against the door. "Meteor shower, guys!"

Oh no. I look out the window and see the burning rocks falling down from the sky, leaving those distinctive and now-familiar trails. Needless to say, they can do some real damage.

We're safer in the rover than we would be out in the open, but it also isn't built to withstand a pounding forever. One of the meteorites hits the ground right next to us, spraying sand at the rover. I instinctively flinch, even though it doesn't hit us.

"Hold on," Errol says grimly, the sound of meteors hitting the sand around us punctuating his words. The rover rocks as one hits us directly, the boom of it hitting the metal rever-berating through the vehicle. "There is a ridge over to the right that we can take cover in."

He floors the accelerator, and we jerk forward.

There's no avoiding bumping into Melchior now. In fact, he deliberately presses me back against the seat with one muscled arm, holding me in place as Errol drives hard and fast towards the ridge. This is what I get for praying for some distance from Melchior. That's not what I meant, Tajss!

I grip his forearm, squeezing my eyes shut at the dizzying

speed and the blur of the landscape through the window. The meteors continue to pelt us, the banging loud enough that I worry they're doing real damage to the rover.

"Almost there!" Errol calls back, his voice grim.

The rover jerks and then skids. I squeeze my eyes shut even tighter, bracing for impact...but it never comes. After a moment, I also realize meteorites are no longer hitting the rover.

I open my eyes cautiously and look around. We're under the ridge that Errol must have been talking about. The rover's side is a few yards away from a wall of reddish rock that continues up to form a wide overhang, wide enough to cover the entire rover. The sound of the meteorites hitting the sand out in the open desert is still clear, but a lot more muted now that we're not directly under them.

When I look back out into the desert, it looks almost apocalyptic, the sky literally raining fire down on Tajss. I suppress a shiver at the thought.

The sound of our harsh breathing echoes inside the confines of the vehicle.

"Okay," Kate mutters, breaking the silence. "Looks like we're going to be waiting this out here."

The pragmatic words bring me back down to earth. Or Tajss.

Errol lets out a huff of breath. "Yes," he agrees. Leaning forward, he cranes his neck to look around. "There are caverns we can move to. Depending on the length of the shower, we may be forced to camp here for the night."

Great. This is so not what I meant when I was praying about being able to get some space between Melchior and me. But there you go—that's life.

Within short order, we're all loaded down with supplies and pallets, standing outside the rover, careful to stay under the overhang. The last thing we need is to accidentally poke an elbow out there right now.

When we step into the first cavern, the space that can be occupied comfortably is quite small, the ceiling angling down in the back.

"Perhaps you and Kate can take this one, and Addison and I can settle into the other," Melchior suggests. "We will all be more comfortable."

I don't know about that. But I can't argue that we'll all at least have more space.

"All right," Kate murmurs, looking around as she drops her bundle onto the ground. "I guess we'll all meet up again when the meteor shower is over. Or in the morning if we end up having to stay the night."

Errol looks out of the cave opening, nodding.

"Yes. For now, it is best we take this opportunity to rest."

With a promise to see them soon, Melchior and I head out of their cavern and into the one next door. It's about the same size, with the ceiling above just tall enough for Melchior to stand in, at least in the front. It tapers lower in the back as well, creating a more confined space. We stick to the front.

Melchior stakes out his area, a couple yards in from the cave opening.

"I think it is best if you set your pallet directly behind my own," he says, eyeing the opening and the cave itself.

I nod. I know why he wants to set things up like this. This way he can be between any danger and me, and he wants me close in case he has to grab me. I have the shock stick, but I definitely feel a lot safer with him between me and the rest of Tajss. It's probably unrealistic to feel like he can take on an army by himself, but that's how I feel. Along with a glow of warmth in my chest at the fact that he cares, that his first thought is to ensure I'm safe. Then again, maybe he would do the same for everyone and I'm reading too much into it?

I'm sick of my own thoughts at this point. Sometimes I feel like I'm going crazy with this back-and-forth in my head when it comes to us. I roll out my pallet, brooding about that.

When I look up, my eye goes to Melchior. He sets up his area efficiently, his pallet much larger to accommodate his height, his muscled frame...

Great, I'm eyeing him again, and now it's worse because we're actually alone, with nowhere else to be, and nothing else to do. I rub my hands on my thighs, feeling nerves and desire mix inside me. This is actually way worse than being in the car. I don't know if I'm going to be able to sleep if we do end up having to stay the night.

"Addison?"

"Hmm?"

I look up from where I've been hyper focused on smoothing out one of the corners of the pallet. Anything to try to get my mind off of him. It wasn't really helping.

When I look up, it's to find Melchior has closed the distance between us. When he crouches down to be more level with me, my heart gives a hard thud. This close up, I can see every eyelash, can see just how ridiculously green his eyes are. How soft his hair looks. My eyes drop to his mouth, but I yank them up again almost immediately. Only to find his eyes focused on my mouth.

I swallow, feeling myself start to sweat for an entirely different reason than the heat of Tajss' suns. When his eyes move back up to meet mine, I can almost feel the banked heat in them.

"I cannot continue to avoid how I feel," he says bluntly.

Thump, thump, thump. My heart is beating so hard at this point I'm almost surprised I'm still upright. I have to form a coherent answer now, his expectant air forcing me to strong some words together somehow.

I clear my throat.

"How...do you feel?" I ask, my voice slightly hoarse.

I need this to be clear. I don't think I'm reading the signals wrong, but...

"There is something between us, some connection that I cannot explain away. Even before the dream..." He shakes his head. "I want you, Addison." The words, in that husky, deep voice, send a shiver through me. "Do you want me?"

His eyes are direct, his gaze clear. Vulnerable. He's willing to put himself out there like this, willing to be hurt. I know how much courage that takes. Honestly...in that moment, I can't remember why I ever thought this wasn't a good idea.

There is a connection between us. One that I can't explain completely deny. I want him. Want him so much now that it actually hurts.

"Yes," I murmur.

Yes. And that's it. That one small word seals the deal.

Melchior reaches out for me and I go willingly into his arms.

He stands up with me in them, carries me back to his pallet, and sets me down on it gently. His eyes are focused, intense, as he reaches for my shirt, stripping it off me in economical motions. Then my pants, my shoes. My bra and underwear follow suit.

His eyes devour me, glittering and hot while he works on his own clothes, stripping them off even faster than my own, his hands much less careful.

I resist the urge to cover myself. It helps that I have him to focus on.

And I have to say...wow.

There's no hiding the strength, the raw power in that body.

The breadth of his shoulders, those biceps, the heaviness of his chest and the hard stomach. His thighs and calves are like-wise thick with muscle, his body framed by his folded wings.

I don't have a lot of time to admire the masterpiece that is his body. As soon as he's completely stripped down, he layers his body over mine, making room for himself between my legs, propping himself up on his forearms so he doesn't crush me.

The first time we kiss is with full body contact. Full, naked body contact.

It's almost too much after all the waiting, all the lost sleep, all the questioning of what's between us. It's straight from zero to a hundred.

I moan as his lips settle over mine, soft and firm and commanding. His hands cup my head, angling me so he can kiss me deeper, his tongue slipping into my mouth. My hands slide up those hard arms, up to grip his shoulders as I kiss him back.

I feel like I've been thrown right into the deep end, but I don't want to be saved. I want to sink in. My hands slide down his flanks, down to cup the hard curve of his butt. Yeah, I want to stay right here, thanks.

I shift under him, my rock-hard nipples scraping against him, sending a sizzle of sensation through me. We're just kissing, but I feel that hot, wet contact everywhere.

Melchior tilts his head, biting gently at my lower lip, making teasing forays before deepening the kiss once more. He settles into it like he loves the act of kissing, like he's in no rush to go anywhere else just yet.

Until my legs are moving restlessly underneath him, my hips arching to rub up against the erection I can feel pressed against me. I want to see it. Want to hold it. Want him to touch me...everywhere.

When he finally breaks the kiss, I'm almost whimpering in need, my fingernails digging into his hips.

"Melchior..."

"Shh. I need to touch you, taste you," he growls, sliding his face down my neck to kiss my shoulder, suck on this skin there. I arch up at the hot suction, wanting that sensation in a few more key places.

It's like he hears that request.

He kisses his way down to my collar bones, taking his time to trail gentle, suckling kisses along them. Who knew collarbones could be such a source of pleasure? I certainly had no idea.

He rises up to look down at me.

Well, my breasts, more specifically.

"Mmm," escapes my mouth as he brings his large calloused hands up to cup them, kneading and squeezing, his gaze fascinated.

I gasp when one of his thumbs grazes my nipples. He looks up at my face for a moment before turning his attention back down and lowering his head to take one stiff peak into his warm mouth. I arch up into the firm suction he applies, feeling the tug almost as strongly between my legs as I do at my nipple.

My hands slide into his hair as he licks at me, suckles at me, then switches over to the other breast, his hands still cupping and squeezing them as though he can't get enough.

I am so fine with that.

He stays there, switching between my breasts, alternating those long hard sucks with gentle kisses and light nibbles. Until I don't know if I want him to stop or go on forever.

My hands clench tightly in his hair when he finally rubs his face against them, my body almost trembling with antici-pation, a slick sheen of sweat covering all of me.

He kisses his way down my stomach, moving as slowly as

ever, as if he's savoring every moment, committing it to memory. While I go completely crazy under him. Not that I'm complaining.

His hands slide under my thighs and lift them up, setting them over his shoulders.

I look down.

His eyes are completely focused on the most intimate part of me, his mouth red and swollen from working my body over already. His thumbs grip me and pull me apart, the fire in his eyes so hot now I almost wonder at the fact that I don't burn under his regard.

"You are...so beautiful," he murmurs, his eyes coming up to meet mine. "I have to..."

My breath catches in my throat when he leans down.

And licks me. A long, slow, thorough taste that has my toes curling and my head dropping back down to the soft pallet in self-defense. I can't watch while he does that. The visual coupled with the sensation is just...yeah. I shut my eyes tight while he licks at me. Every inch of me down there, his hands gripping my thighs and keeping them wide when I start to close them, the feelings so sharp I almost can't handle them.

Then he finds my clit.

I jump when he flicks his tongue over it and I can feel him pause. Assess. Then he places his mouth there and stays there. I cry out as he sucks at me, his tongue lapping against me. My hands clench, my thighs try to close again...

And the orgasm hits me like a freight train.

My body arches, the waves of pleasure hitting me one after the other. Melchior stays glued to me, his mouth stays exactly where it needs to be to keep the climax going, way longer than I thought it could. Until I finally fall limp, my breath coming in gasps. I feel like I've been taken apart and put back together, just slightly differently than before.

I slowly open my eyes when Melchior kisses my inner thigh and rises up, my legs falling to either side of his hips.

My eyes scan down his body...to his erection.

And I freeze.

That is...large. I blink. Thick and long and trembling with his pulse, the head is already wet with arousal.

Melchior stills when I sit up and reach out to grip it, the thickness and heft of it sending a thrill of awareness through me, and some trepidation.

He's huge, which I guess is expected given his size, but knowing that and seeing it are so not the same thing. When I run my thumb along the top, I also feel the ridges and that last bump at the base that I've heard rumors of—rumors that have all been complimentary, but I have to say, seeing the size now...

"Addison," Melchior growls. "I do not want to release in your hand."

I start, realizing the whole time I've been thinking, I've also been sliding my hand up and down his length, rubbing my thumb over his leaking head.

Oops.

Pushing me gently back down onto the pallet, he reaches down to grip his erection in his own hand. That looks...nice.

I lick my lips, my hands gripping his forearms.

"Go slow, Melchior," I warn.

His face softens at the request. He leans down to kiss me.

"Do not worry," he reassures me, his tip just kissing me lower down on my body. "I will be careful."

I nod, taking a deep breath as he starts to push into me. It's tight—very tight. But I'm so wet and he's so careful, that I only feel that distinct pressure, that feeling of being stretched.

He watches me as he slowly works his way into me,

gentle thrusts in and out. Making room for himself inside. I take a deep breath, trying to relax underneath him to help.

He reaches between us, and his fingers get to work, rubbing, drawing circles. I sigh, closing my eyes as he finally pushes all the way inside, his hips pressing against mine. I'm so full I feel like I can feel him in my throat, but I'm adjusting to him. I love the feeling of his heartbeat inside me, love having him above me and around me like this.

"Good?" he murmurs, his hand cupping my face.

I nod, sighing.

"Yes." I open my eyes, smiling at him as I raise my legs to wrap around his hips. "But I think you should move."

Concern gives way to that now-familiar fire, and he gives me exactly what I ask for. Pulling out slowly, he pushes back in just as leisurely, and I get a good feel of just what those ridges can do. Watching me, gauging my reactions, he angles my hips so every single one hits me just right. All the way up until the one at his base that grinds against me...oh...so...good.

I feel the pleasure start to build again, which is honestly a surprise. I didn't think I could go again. But it builds as I feel him move inside me, his body shifting in a wave of rippling muscle, his eyes scanning my body, the desire in them calling my own.

His eyes lock on where our bodies meet, watching as he pistons in and out of me, faster now that I've relaxed around him. Then his attention turns to my breasts, swaying with each inward thrust.

Sliding his hands up, he cups them, thumbing the nipples. And then leans down to take a tip in his mouth. I push my hips back up against him, wrapping my arms around him and holding on tight as he builds up the force of his thrusts, his body sliding along the front of mine.

I feel so completely taken over in the most delicious way

possible. He lets go of my breast and brings his mouth down on mine, his hips still moving as we kiss. He pushes into me hard, grinding against me.

I cry out into his mouth at the unexpected force of the sensation, pushing back against him, my body as tight as a bow as I come again. He shudders above me as I clench down on him, squeezing him rhythmically as the pleasure rides me once more. His hoarse moan clues me in before he jerks inside me, following me over that delicious edge, his muscled body trembling above my own.

I hold him tight, kissing his jaw, his neck, his shoulders as he slowly comes back down. With a sigh, I fall back on the pallet again. I'm so...relaxed. I rub my face against the side of Melchior's neck, my legs falling off of his hips.

But then I feel something else stir, poke at my thigh. I freeze as Melchior rises up once more. I know exactly what I'm going to see when I look down. His second penis, the one that stays tucked under his tail until the first is...done I guess. I know about it, but I still stare.

"I don't know Melchior," I murmur. "I'm wrung out."

He smiles at me, reaching out to flip me over onto my stomach. Is it weird that I find his strength so hot?

"Do not worry," he reassures me, lifting my hips up. "I will do all the work."

And then he slides into me. I cry out at the harsh pleasure, my body already sensitive from the two earlier orgasms. It feels...amazing.

I rest the side of my face on the pallet, bracing myself as Melchior thrusts into me, using a measured, slow pace. I feel like I'm having a continuous, low-grade orgasm the whole time, all of my nerve endings firing at once. As Melchior thrusts carefully into me, I luxuriate in the sensations, even as I wonder why the heck I waited so long to feel this. The ride is slower, gentler this time, both of us having taken the edge off, but it's no less mind melting. By the time Melchior comes again, I'm twisting in pleasure under him, the orgasm deep and almost gradual in its onset.

This time, both of us fall limply onto the pallet afterwards. I don't think I could lift my pinkie if my life depended on it. I vaguely feel Melchior gather me close and kiss my forehead, but my body decides it's had enough. It's lights out for me between one breath and the next.

I'm sure there's a ridiculous smile on my face as I drift off.

10

MELCHIOR

I fall asleep with Addison in my arms and feel as though I am dreaming. This is so much more than I thought I could have. I can hardly believe that she is lying here with me. When I wake up with her still here, I know I want this every day. Want her by my side.

But I can hear the meteorite shower has ended. We must leave soon, even though what I want is to stay here with Addison in my arms. I watch her sleeping face for a moment more. She appears softer, more vulnerable, her shields not up yet to guard herself from the world. I smooth a hand down her back and kiss her forehead, reluctant to wake her when she seems so peaceful.

But we need to go.

"Addison. We must depart," I murmur.

She sighs, her eyes blinking open, focusing on me. I feel the moment she is awake, her entire body tensing against my own. She sits up, a pretty flush coloring her cheeks when she realizes she is unclothed.

"Uh, okay. I'll just get dressed then," she mutters, reaching out for her clothing.

I have the urge to pull her back towards me, to soothe her sudden anxiety, but then I hear Errol call out for us.

"Addison, Melchior—it is time to continue!"

Addison is dressed so quickly that I have to blink. That was...very fast. I follow suit in a slightly less manic manner, and we pack everything up together. I want to say more, want to have a moment to ourselves, but there is no time. We must leave.

I feel somewhat disgruntled at that as we exit the cave, Kate and Errol are already ready and waiting for us at the rover. But, once again, duty calls.

"I hope that is the last meteor shower we encounter for the rest of the journey," Errol remarks while we secure our belongings in the rover.

I nod. The delay may already have cost the settlement. Even though I recognize that, I find it difficult to regret it, not when I spent the time with Addison in my arms.

But it does mean that we must hurry. Without any more discussion, we sit down in the rover and continue on our way. The earlier tension between Addison and me has dissipated. I adjust myself discreetly when an image flashes in my mind, a reminder of just why that particular tension is gone.

I glance over at Addison to see her looking out the window, her demeanor contemplative. Is she thinking of last night too? I cannot address it now, not with others in the car.

There is not much conversation in any case, not when with all of us focused on what we may encounter at our destination. We do not have much farther to travel.

Cognizant of that fact, the anxiety level in the vehicle begins to rise as we near the settlement. What will we find? Were they able to hold off the attack? We won't know until we arrive.

"We're here," Kate announces in a tense voice. "Just over this rise."

I lean forward to see through the windshield in the front.

"Oh no!" Addison gasps, looking ahead.

"Shit," Kate mutters.

Yes. I clench my jaw as I take in the scene.

The settlement is currently under attack, a small army of the invaders already encroaching upon its borders. It is clear the humans are having trouble holding them back, even with Zmaj help.

The distinctive flash of a lochaber catches my eye and I see Ragnar kill two of the invaders with one well-timed blow. After I see him, I can pick out Ryuth and Padraig spread along the line of defense, fighting with grim determination. They are excellent warriors, but there are not enough of them to hold back that many of the attackers alone.

I tense when I hear a loud bang. One of the invaders jerks in response and falls back.

"They have remnants of the guns from the ship, but they don't have any means to recharge them!" Kate shouts as we near, the din of battle making hearing her more difficult. "I'm guessing that's why they aren't just shooting out there willy-nilly!"

I scan the battle, feeling my stomach roll at the thought of Addison anywhere near the bloody mess.

"Errol," I say.

He nods, glancing over at Kate.

"I am going to drive through them. Hold on."

I brace myself, making sure to extend my arm in front of Addison to hold her in place too.

Errol slams his foot down on the accelerator and the rover leaps forward, right through a group of the invaders trying to enter the settlement. Some of them scatter just in time, but we run over more than a few, the bumps and staccato screams a clear indicator.

Pushing the brakes once we are through, Errol turns the steering wheel to bring the rover to a rocking stop right in front of a group of huddled human females, their eyes wide as they take us in.

"Addison, you and Kate stay here with the others," I order, opening the door.

"Okay," she agrees, not arguing.

Kate does not either, stepping out of the car with Addison. Errol and I abandon the rover as well. It was useful to get into the settlement, to leave Addison and Kate in a safer spot, but it is not practical to try to kill more of the invaders with it. Not when some of our own people are out there. There is too much of a chance that we may accidentally hit one of them in an attack.

We attack as we normally would. Lochaber in hand, we waste no time before joining the melee.

Taking a running leap, I swing my weapon in a hard arc in front of me, wounding multiple attackers at once and clearing a space to fight within.

One of those I cut in the initial attack growls, the sound oddly spaced just as their roars are. The cold hate I see in its full black eyes does not surprise me. I think the invaders came to Tajss with the idea that they would find easy prey here. Having us protect the humans really does interfere with those plans, and I have no problem with that.

Even if we weren't creating a new society together, I wouldn't want any sentient, intelligent creatures being taken as slaves. So I simply jerk my head at the angry invader, goading him to attack me—and he does. I dodge the blow he attempts to land, sweeping his legs out from under him. He manages to slash at my leg, but he's dead in the next moment.

Just as I stagger forward from an attack from the rear. Growling myself now, I fling my new opponent off my back, using the blunt end of my lochaber to push my attacker away.

When I glance up briefly, I meet Addison's eyes. They are focused fully on me while she huddles with the other women watching the fight.

But I do not have time to more than glance at her as three other invaders attempt a concerted attack upon me.

My muscles burn as I continue to battle, using my lochaber to keep some distance, leaping into the air and using vertical space to avoid swipes with their weapons and hands. I land once more, crouching low and ready for another attack when a human runs up from behind us. A male.

"One of the women has been taken!" he yells. "They went that way!"

"We shall find her!" Ragnar returns immediately, taking Padraig's arm and running in the direction the male pointed to. If they do not retrieve her before they secure her in their ship, she may soon be off world and out of reach.

I look over at Ryuth as I try to catch my breath, only to find him looking back at me. He nods at me, gripping his gore-covered lochaber in his hands. Jackson, the human male seemingly in charge here at the settlement, steps forward as well with his group. We will have to hold the line without the others' help now.

The invaders attack with a renewed burst of energy when they see the Zmaj numbers have been cut down. But we do not give in.

I enter that mental arena, that cold, quiet place where fighting is second nature. Dodge, leap, stab, sweep. My muscles have their own memory, react almost on their own as I fight invader after invader, ignoring the pain of minor wounds and bruises.

The battle is arduous, but the front line has already done

much of the work before we even arrived. The invaders that are attacking are dangerous, but I can sense the weakness in them. For the most part, they have lost that gleam of confidence in their eyes, that surety that they believe their tricks will work. It is more a battle of endurance at this point than anything else. And endure we do.

It takes time, my body continuing to move long after I feel the pull of exhaustion. We cannot stop. If we stop, not only will we be taken or killed, but those depending on us will be kidnapped as well.

Addison's face hovers in my mind's eyes, motivating me to hit with the same force, dodge with the same swiftness even though I am tiring. I refuse to give in. And that perseverance prevails.

The battle eventually ends, most of the invaders dead at our feet, others escaping, deciding to retreat. We stay in place a bit longer, ensuring others will not arrive, that this is not another trick they are attempting to use on us. But it is not. No others appear.

I catch my breath, turning to ensure the women are whole and healthy. They are, including Addison. I do not go to her, though I have a strong urge to do that.

Now that we have space and time, we take the opportunity to confer with the patrols on site.

"What other areas may be vulnerable?" I ask, Ryuth by my side.

"The flanks," Jackson returns, his face flushed and gleaming with sweat. "I'll show you."

We do a sweep of the vulnerable portions of the mining settlement, attempting to root out any invaders lying in wait while also devising a defensive plan. My mind should be firmly on the task at hand, but thoughts of Addison seep in throughout.

I feel my impatience, ignited by my desire to go back to

her. After what we shared in that cave, our link has deepened. Neither of us know what the true implications of that change are. I worry at that thought while I try to focus on the defenses.

When we finally accomplish everything we need to ensure the settlement's safety, I almost run back to where I left Addison, eager to see her. She is not quite where I left her after that much time, but I find her easily enough, just in time for the heavily guarded communal meal.

"Are you all right?" she asks when I approach, looking me over in concern.

"Yes, only minor wounds and bruises. Are you well?"

She appears fine and whole, as expected. I would never have left with the others to secure the settlement's flanks otherwise.

"Yes," she sighs, her bottom lip poking out. "I wish I'd been more of a help though."

I shake my head, taking her hand in mine to lead her over to the communal meal.

"The best thing you could have done was stay out of danger. When another woman was taken by the invaders, it forced us to split our numbers. Never good during a battle."

She sobers, nodding.

"True." I see her glance around at the assembled people. "Why are we eating outside? Shouldn't we be under cover just in case?"

"It was Jackson's idea," I explain as we take a seat at a table that is already half full. "He thought eating outside in clear sight would send a message."

"That we're easy targets?" she quips.

I chuckle, shaking my head.

"No, that we are not afraid. Perhaps if we show no fear, the invaders will reconsider any attacks during the night. He thinks a show of confidence might make them wonder if we have something else at our disposal they do not know about."

"Hmm." She turns her eyes back to me. "Do you think that's a good idea?"

"Perhaps." I point discretely to where people are stationed, both humans and Zmaj. "The area is being carefully guarded. If it does not work, we will not be caught unawares."

She nods.

"All right, I guess that makes sense."

Errol and Kate arrive and the conversation shifts to something much more interesting.

"Seems like this may not have been an attack just to take people," Kate murmurs as she sits down next to us, her eyes scanning the area. "They've found some new ore in the mines. Might be the reason for this particular assault on the settlement."

"What kind of ore?" I ask, frowning. "What could they want that badly?"

"Vanadium," Errol responds.

I sit back in my chair at that. This does change things.

"Vanadium?" I repeat.

Addison looks between the two of us.

"Vanadium? What is that? And why would the invaders want it?"

"It is an ore with electrical properties that can be quite useful," I explain, tapping my fingers on the table. "Have you seen it?" I ask Errol. "Does it appear to be so?"

It is a very distinctive ore. He nods.

"A deep red, so deep it is almost black. I cannot be certain, but it appeared to reflect a violet color."

I nod, staring down at the table. This could change a very great deal.

"Electrical properties?" Addison asks, focusing on exactly the right thing.

"Yes," I confirm, meeting her eyes.

I can see the dawning excitement in them. She understands exactly what this could mean. Our conversation is cut short, however, when the food arrives and more people fill in the empty section of the table.

By silent agreement, we focus on the meal and on lighter topics while we eat. Better not to accidentally say something that might have unintended political ramifications. The people here have grudgingly accepted some kind of working relationship with us, but that does not mean they are happy about it.

Despite our decision to keep the conversation light, the dinner is somewhat tense. The knowledge of our vulnerability is not far from anyone's mind. Luckily, despite that edge to the meal, nothing happens. Nobody attacks from the dark of night. We do not have to abandon the tables and draw our weapons mid-bite. We finish the meal in peace.

Everyone decides it is time to retire directly after. It is not late, but a fight such as that is draining. When Addison and I leave the communal dinner, we find quarters for the night together. Neither of us speaks of it. It is simply assumed that we will be together tonight.

Once inside, we lay out our pallets. But when Addison tries to set her own some distance from mine, I pull it over so it's right next to it instead, creating a larger one for both of us to use together. She looks up at me, biting her lip.

"Addison," I murmur, reaching out slowly to draw her into my arms. She comes easily, sighing as she rests her head against my chest, wrapping her arms around my waist. I rest my head against hers, tightening my arms.

"I did not like having you so close to the battle. All I could think of was what would happen to you if we failed to hold the front line," I murmur into her hair.

She draws back so she can look up at me.

"Well, I didn't particularly like to see you in the thick of it," she points out. "Feeling helpless is not all that great either."

I nod. I suppose that is true. I shake my head, reaching up to cup the side of her face with one hand.

"You are right," I concede, looking into her lovely eyes. "But I do not want to think of it anymore. We are alive and together. I want to enjoy that victory..."

When I lean down, she rises up on her toes to meet my kiss. I sigh in pleasure. This is what I've been wanting ever since we left that cave. I reach down to cup her curvy backside in my hands so I can lift her up to a comfortable height. Her lips are soft, gentle against my own.

I carefully drop down onto the pallet with her still held in my arms, not breaking the kiss. She tugs at my clothes impatiently, but I am more than happy to oblige the silent request. I break the kiss to remove them quickly. She does the same, but I am done first, so I move to help her with her shirt.

As soon as it is out of the way, I cup the soft curves of her breasts, tipped with soft pink nipples. I cannot help but stare.

"I would keep you unclothed always if I could," I confess, squeezing her gently. "You are so beautiful."

She smiles, reaching down to run a finger over my member. I close my eyes at the light touch, my body moving towards it of its own accord.

"You aren't so bad yourself," she murmurs.

My eyes drift open. "I want to be inside you."

Her smile fades, her eyes darkening. "Then come here."

I do not go slowly. Laying my body over hers, I reach between her legs, my fingers encountering her wetness.

"I'm ready," she breathes into my ear, biting down gently on the lobe. "Come inside."

My body trembles at the invitation.

Reaching between us, I angle myself, seeking her soft, warm entrance. I rise up on my forearms so I can meet her eyes as I slowly sink into her. They lose focus, her mouth slightly parted, her eyes half closed.

Then I start to move. Slow, languorous thrusts, our bodies sliding against each other perfectly. I watch her the entire time. The way her face flushes. How her hair frames her face, the slight messiness of it more appealing somehow. The water that glimmers over her skin as she grows more heated, as she nears her pleasure...

When she reaches her climax, her head falls back, a low moan leaving her lips, and she squeezes down on me with those delicate muscles. I groan, my hands clenching into fists as I join her. Watching her, feeling her clench down on me, all of it is too much.

But when I close my eyes to enjoy the moment, to revel in it as I desire, I do not see darkness. A burst of light appears instead. And then a view of...the city? As soon as I recognize it, the view shifts once more.

This time to a dark cave, rushing through narrow tunnels, stopping abruptly in front of a rocky wall, flickers of light from a torch highlighting the craggy surface...and a deep vein of rich red.

Vanadium.

As soon as I recognize it, the image slowly fades to show the city once more. And then...black.

My eyes snap open to meet Addison's own wide-eyed gaze.

"The city?" she asks, clearly shaken.

I nod, my jaw tight. "And vanadium," I add.

"We need to take the vanadium to the city," she murmurs, certainty in her voice. "Quickly."

I nod, the same sense of urgency beating inside me. The vision was simple but the message clear, and I have no intention of disregarding it.

Not now.

Not after everything I have seen.

11

ADDISON

*T*he vision infuses both of us with a sense of urgency that we convey to Errol and Kate right away.

"A vision?" Errol repeats, frowning. "You are certain?"

"Yes," Melchior says firmly.

"We both experienced it," I add. "And there was a definite sense that we're short on time. That it's imperative we take the ore back to the city as soon as possible."

"I believe you." Kate rubs my arm, looking over at Errol. "How soon can we leave? And will we be able to take some of the vanadium with us or will that be a problem?"

Errol shakes his head.

"I do not think Jackson will be resistant to the idea, not when the end result may very well be exactly what they need here as well. If we can find a way for the ore to work with the meteorite glass..."

"We could solve the problem with the shields," I finish, nodding. "If we can buy enough time to run the experiments we need," I add.

Even if this is the solution we've all been praying to find, it'll take some time to find a way to make it work.

"Yes," Errol agrees. "Unfortunately, we cannot leave quite yet. We need to be here if the invaders decide to attack again during the night. And traveling during the day is much safer in any case."

"Yes," Melchior murmurs. "That is true. I think it is best we speak with Jackson at dawn then, so as not to waste any time."

On that we can all agree.

Melchior and I head back to the neighboring building and bunk down for the night, forced to wait. I worry that I'm going to have trouble sleeping, but when Melchior pulls me into his arms snugly, it doesn't take long for the figurative lights to go out. That hasn't failed to relax me into sleep yet.

We're ready to go at dawn, as per the plan.

Jackson is already awake, his bloodshot eyes showing the accumulation of sleepless nights.

The stress of the situation would get to anyone. I don't envy him the responsibility of leadership here.

"You need the red ore?" he asks. "What did you call it?"

" Vanadium," Melchior repeats. "And yes—we believe it may be the solution to the shields we are looking for."

"If we can take some of it back to the city with us, we might be able to figure out a way to ensure the shields are actually reliable," I throw in. He needs to see how this would be beneficial to their settlement as well.

Jackson nods, his expression thoughtful. I know he must be considering the merits of just handing the stuff over. The only leverage they have is the mines here. Then again, if they don't get proper shields and the invaders keep attacking, there may not be a settlement that needs protection in the future. Leverage isn't all that important if you're in the position of trying to ensure your survival.

"All right," he agrees. "We have a bunch of it stored in one of the more damaged buildings. You can take what you can carry—I'll have some of the guys help you." He gestures for us to follow him.

He leads us through the settlement and towards the edge in the back. Most everyone is still asleep this early, but there are a couple of men up and guarding the building he leads us to. Seems like a good precaution, considering the timing of the attack. If the invaders want the ore, I think it's safe to assume we don't want them to have it.

The miners look over at us when Jackson tells them we're going to be taking some of the ore. I can't tell what they think of it from their expressions, but neither of them argues when Jackson asks them to help.

"I'll go bring the rover over," Kate announces. "Doesn't make much sense to carry it all the way over to the front if I can just drive it back here."

She hurries away to do that while Jackson and the two men open the door leading inside. The place is filled with the ore, heaps of shining dark red, almost black chunks, the light glinting off it in a lavender shift. When we step in, the air feels like it has almost a charge to it.

"Careful," Jackson warns. "We already—"

A cry of pain interrupts him. Melchior and Errol immediately turn at the sound, their lochabers at the ready. But there is no threat to fight. One of the miners is on the floor, moaning. The other hurries over, admonishing him.

"You have to use cloth, you idiot!" he hisses, kneeling down next to him to check him over.

"Is he okay?" Jackson demands.

"I'm okay," the man answers for himself, slowly sitting up. "My mistake," he adds, holding his head.

Jackson shakes his own head, sighing.

"The ore can give off electricity," he explains. "Enough to

110

give you a good jolt. After a couple people were randomly shocked by the stuff, I instituted a rule—everyone is supposed to have a cloth barrier between their hands and the ore."

Jeez. "Seems like a smart precaution," I murmur.

"I have some empty boxes from the last shipment of supplies that you can use to carry it out," Jackson offers.

"Thank you. We shall need them," Errol murmurs, watching the shocked miner get back to his feet. He's a little wobbly, but seems like he's shaking it off okay. Note to self—do not touch the stuff directly.

When Kate arrives with the rover, we all start to pack the ore into the boxes, using the crude mitts they've devised to get the job done. We're actually able to stack quite a few of the full boxes in the back of the rover, which is good. I don't know how much we'll need, but better we have too much than not enough. By the time Errol and Melchior take out the last of the boxes we're able to fit in the vehicle, some of the other miners are up and watching us load up. I overhear a few snippets of conversation nearby.

"...might be able to help with the shields..."

"...I sure would sleep better with some protection..."

"...I hope they're not just robbing us blind..."

Huh. Good with some suspicion mixed in. The best we could hope for, really.

"Thank you for your help," Jackson offers when we're ready to climb into the rover. "And I hope the ore is helpful."

"We'll let you know when we figure out how to use it," I say, climbing in. "It's going to be our priority when we get back."

He nods, stepping back out of the way. "Have a safe journey."

We thank him for the well wishes, and then Kate slowly

eases the rover forward through the settlement, careful to give people ample time to move out of the way.

Within minutes, we're out of the settlement and in the open desert once more. I look back at the boxes piled high behind us. They're covered in a thick tarp for extra protection.

"I really hope this ore is the answer we're looking for," I say, turning back around. "The shields are obviously the top priority. But if we can figure out how to make them work with the vanadium, maybe we can also use the ore as a power source for the old tech in the city."

"Yes," Errol agrees from beside Kate. "That possibility has crossed my mind as well. We will begin testing as soon as we can."

I nod, smiling at Melchior when he reaches over to take my hand. I squeeze it tightly, hope blooming in my chest.

"I am so up for some cool new tech," Kate says, grinning as she maneuvers deftly around some stray rocks. "Maybe we can figure out some air conditioning or something!"

I laugh. "That would be a game changer," I admit. "I'm keeping all my fingers and toes crossed."

Melchior smiles at me, and the hope melds with a warm feeling of happiness. For once, everything actually feels pretty damn perfect. I cover Melchior's hand with my free one, marveling at the fact that I can feel this way on Tajss of all places. I would never have predicted it.

There was a time, not all that long ago, when I thought all hope was lost. That we'd be stuck in that tunnel underground with Annabel for the rest of our sad lives. And, more recently, that Melchior only wanted to be friends. That I'd be stuck perpetually pining after the unattainable.

Now, I'm not only living in a proper city, we might actually get the old tech there running properly! And I have someone who seems to want to be with me, someone who makes me feel sappy when I think of him. I so didn't expect to find myself here. I feel almost giddy with hope, despite all of the problems we're currently facing.

Of course, that's exactly when Tajss decides it's the perfect time to throw another wrench in the works. I should know better now than to entertain any optimism!

It starts with a slight rocking of the rover, one that I dismiss, attributing it to driving over rocks.

Then the rocking intensifies, and we actually start to skid sideways. Yeah, rocks can't do that.

"Shit!" Kate mutters through gritted teeth, trying to get control of the rover once more. "What the hell is that? An earthquake?"

"Zemlja," Melchior says grimly.

"Yes. Stop the vehicle, Kate," Errol barks.

My stomach drops. Zemlja. Not good news.

I jerk in my seat when the sand in front of us bursts open in a spattering spray that hits the windshield hard. The thing that shoots out is something out of a nightmare. Thick and segmented, it looks like a giant earthworm with scales, the fleshy color oddly disgusting. Unfortunately, the end isn't closed off like an earthworm. The head curves down and the mouth opens some yards away, though it's still close enough, thank you very much.

My eye goes straight to the teeth revealed by that gaping mouth, concentric rings of sharp white fangs that go all the way down into its gullet. As if that isn't enough, it spits something at us that doesn't quite reach the rover. I don't know what that liquid is, but when it hits the sand, it smokes and sizzles. Acid spit? Like it already isn't monster enough!?

"Stay in the rover!" Melchior orders as both he and Errol fling their doors open.

Copy that. I have no desire to go out there.

"Shit, that thing is huge," Kate mutters while we watch

Errol and Melchior approach from opposite sides, lochabers ready in hand.

"Yeah," I breathe, clenching my hands as Melchior gets closer.

I don't want him that close to the thing, but I also have a feeling we won't be getting away without confronting it. I hold my breath as I watch Melchior twirl his lochaber like it weighs nothing, when I know for a fact it's difficult for me to even hold, it's so damn heavy. He walks in front of the zemlja, still twirling his weapon like he doesn't have a care in the world.

What's he doing?

I gasp when the thing lunges at him, cobra quick, my hands reaching forward to grip the seats. But Melchior darts to the side, avoiding the acid spit and the sharp teeth.

Errol takes advantage of the distraction to stab at the thing with his lochaber, aiming for a spot just under its neck. It jerks to the side, blood spraying as it turns to Errol, focused on him now. Melchior takes the opportunity to stab it just under the first wound on the opposite side. It pulls back, lunging once more, but Melchior isn't there again. Working in tandem, Errol and Melchior continue to chip away at it, avoiding lunges and acid almost like they've choreographed the moves. I might have even enjoyed the show if the stakes weren't literally life and death. Instead, I lean forward, flinching every time the thing lunges, every time it spits acid.

"Shit," Kate breathes when Melchior executes a particularly complicated maneuver, sliding under the thing mid-lunge and flipping over to slice at its base.

Well, what we can see anyway. I have no idea how much more of it is under the sand. Isn't that just creepy?

That last slicing wound seems to be the limit for the zemlja. Jerking back, it doesn't lunge again or try to attack with its killer saliva. Instead, it closes its mouth and pulls back into the ground, back through the hole it tunneled to get out to the surface, almost as though it was yanked back in.

Errol and Melchior immediately run back to the rover.

"Go!" Errol shouts before he jumps in. "Before it decides to return!"

Melchior slides in just as Kate floors the accelerator and the rover leaps forward, swerving around the hole.

I tense, looking down at the dark, gaping hole, hoping the thing doesn't decide to pop back out at exactly that moment...

It doesn't. I let out a sigh of relief, sliding over to hug Melchior close. He hugs me back as he catches his breath, kissing the top of my head.

"That was too much excitement," I whisper.

He tightens his hold.

"We are not far from the city now," he reassures me. "I doubt we will encounter more trouble."

I glare up at him.

"You're not supposed to say that," I admonish him. "That's how you jinx us!"

"Jinx?" he repeats, confused.

Kate chuckles. "She means that's how you invite trouble," she explains.

"Ah." His face clears and he smiles. "Then I shall say perhaps the worst is in front of us."

That has me snorting in laughter and Kate cackling in response. Errol shakes his head, grinning as well. The tension well and truly broken, I finally relax a little.

Melchior actually turns out to be right. We reach the city without another incident, but that doesn't mean we can relax.

We have urgent business, so as soon as we stop the rover inside, we rush over to Rosalind's office.

She sees us right away, though I know she's busy with everything she's responsible for here in the city.

I bet Jackson would crumple under the kind of pressure Rosalind is always under, but she looks as serene as always, her dark hair smoothed back in a ponytail, her beautiful face set in calm lines.

Visidion stands behind her, his dark green eyes watchful. Rosalind's mate doesn't play. I know if he perceives any kind of threat towards her, he'll deal with it swiftly and harshly. As a Tribe Commander in his own right, the match is one of equals. I've always admired that.

"You have news?" she asks when we stream into her office.

"Yes," Kate confirms. "The mining settlement was under attack, but the settlers were able to push the invaders back into a retreat with Zmaj help."

"Though they may yet attack again," Errol warns.

Visidion frowns.

"Perhaps it might have been better for you to stay and help...is there a reason you hurried back?"

"Yes," I interject. "The miners found a new kind of ore called vanadium. It might be why the invaders decided to attack them now. Have you heard of it?"

Visidion nods slowly.

"An ore that has...electrical properties if I recall correctly..." His eyes light up with comprehension. "You believe it could help with the shields?"

"Perhaps," Melchior confirms.

"And perhaps it could also help us bring the rest of the old tech here in the city back online," I add, unable to hold back my excitement. "If this stuff works, the sky could be the limit."

"The sky, huh?" Rosalind repeats, a smile flirting with her lips.

"Addison is correct. We wanted to speak with you immediately because..." Melchior glances over at me. "Addison and I shared a vision last night. One that we believe conveyed the message that we needed to return to the city with the ore. There was a sense of urgency in it we could not deny."

Rosalind and Visidion share a glance I can't decipher.

"We want clearance to get to work on the ore immediately," I say into the pause. "Vision or no, it only makes sense to get to try to figure out if this stuff can help us."

Visidion nods and Rosalind turns back to us.

"True." Her eyes linger on me and Melchior, her sharp gaze missing nothing. "You have the clearance. Clean up, eat something, and get to work as soon as you can."

"Yes, ma'am," I murmur.

Excitement beats through my veins as the meeting ends and we leave her office. This is going to be the breakthrough we needed.

It has to be.

MELCHIOR

*W*hen I step into the lab, I find Addison already at one of the tables, focused on the machinery in front of her. A box full of vanadium sits to her right, and a box of meteorite glass is over to her left, both within easy reach. She's frowning, muttering to herself as she works with tweezers and a slim metal tool, hunched over.

She looks adorable.

But she has been working nonstop for too long. I step over towards her and she looks up at the sound.

"Are you making any progress?" I ask, settling a hand on the small of her back.

She lets out a frustrated breath, shaking her head. "No," she responds glumly. "I've tried every hack I can think of, every which way, but still—nothing!" She throws her hands up in frustration, but doesn't let go of her tools, bringing them back down to get back to work. "I'll figure it out," she mutters, fiddling with the small components in front of her. "I just need to keep tinkering with it..."

That's exactly what she doesn't need to do. She needs a break. I can see it in the shadows in her eyes, in the rising frustration at the failed attempts. The problem is, she will not take a break herself.

Fortunately, I know exactly how to push the issue and relieve this tension...

I pick up the stool she is sitting on and turn it so she is facing me rather than the table and the problem she has been worrying at. She blinks up at me with wide eyes while I gently take the tools from her hands and set them down on the table. I take both of her hands and massage them for a moment, feeling the tiny delicate bones there. When she is distracted by my touch, I ease her from the stool.

"Come, Addison. You need a break."

She tries to pull back, realizing I am intending to lead her out of the lab, but I pull her along gently, out of the lab and into one of the smaller store rooms nearby. I glance around before I close the door, ensuring there is nobody nearby.

"Melchior, I can't take a break yet," she insists. "I still haven't tried the resistor—"

Gripping her hips, I lift her up against the wall and set my mouth on hers in a kiss that's immediately deep, wet. She stiffens at the abrupt contact, clearly surprised, but then she sighs, softening against me and raising her hands up to slide them into my hair. I groan at the touch, at the acceptance as her body melds against my own.

I love how she responds to me.

Breaking the kiss, I slide my mouth down her soft throat, pulling the loose neck of her shirt down, taking her under-garment with it to expose one rounded breast. Groaning, I take it into my mouth, sucking hard as I unfasten her pants. As soon as they are open, I yank them down and off, leaving them dangling off one foot. It doesn't matter. They aren't in the way there.

She cries out as I give her breast one last hard suck before kissing my way back up to her neck, biting down gently on her shoulder as I release my hard cock. I put my hand between us to test her readiness, but when I feel her ready slickness, I have to have a taste. I crouch, settling her thighs on my shoulders, and close my mouth over the softest part of her, licking and sucking the way I know she likes it.

Her cry is sharp but short. When I look up, I see her eyes are shut tightly closed and she has covered her mouth with her hand, aware that there might be people close by. The thrill of that knowledge flows through me, heightening every sensation. I lick at her faster, spearing two fingers into her at the same time. Her cry is muffled as she arches into me, her orgasm coming hard and fast.

I drink it down, revel in it, ensure she stays at that glowing peak as long as possible. When she slowly relaxes, I stand, moving her legs so they are locked around my waist, and I push into her in one long thrust. My hands clench on her hips as I try not to make a sound, the feel of her surrounding me so abruptly an intense one.

And so necessary.

She clutches at my shoulders, her chest heaving as she tries to catch her breath. I don't let her. Sliding my arm under her back to buffer her from the hard wall, I pump into her hard and fast. Her head drops against my shoulder, her mouth open against my skin, her hips trying to push against me for more.

It is hot, quick, primal. It's what both of us need after the trip to the mining settlement. A release from the tension, a way to clear the mind before she finds a way to fix the problems that plague us.

And I know she will.

She will find a way to fix the shields, activate the old technology in the city, understand the ever-elusive invaders' vessel. Because she is just that capable, just that intelligent.

But in that moment, inside her, I must confess...I am not thinking of her mind.

This time, she does not reach completion first. Slapping my hand against the wall to brace myself, I squeeze into her tightness as deeply as I can go.

The pleasure is sharp and all encompassing, the quickness of it almost bringing me to my knees.

And then Addison cries out with her own orgasm, squeezing my length, her legs tightening on my waist. I brace my legs, another wave of pleasure going through me as I try to remain upright.

Oh...

I come back slowly, the sound of my breathing and Addison's the only thing I hear in the small room.

"That was...intense," Addison murmurs, sliding her arms around my neck in a hug.

I nod.

In all honesty, I was not expecting something so...primal, and I can sense Addison did not expect it either. I am somewhat shaken by it, by my own behavior. I pride myself on my control, but Addison can so easily take that from me. I lift my head to meet her still-out-of-focus eyes, not knowing exactly what I intend to say. But it does not matter.

A sound has us both freezing in place.

Footsteps.

Familiar ones.

And then the sound of Errol's voice—nearby.

"Where have they gone?" we hear him mutter irritably. "We have so much we need to accomplish!"

Addison and I glance at each other. Her mouth twitches into a smile and I suppress the urge to laugh.

"We better get back," Addison whispers, wiggling to get down.

My eye falls on her still-exposed breast, jiggling from the

motion, and I cannot resist the urge to kiss it. She stills at the touch.

"Mmm."

I rub my face on it before I finally set her down gently, and we quickly right ourselves. My second cock still aches, but I cannot do anything about that now. It will have to wait.

Addison opens the door, looking back at me. She looks up and down the hallway, then turns back to me and gives a tiny nod. I nod in return and follow her out, back to the lab.

When we step back inside, Errol turns to us, his countenance irritated, but his expression changes quickly when he looks us over, the slight scowl shifting into a sly grin. I frown, looking over at Addison. Her hair is a little messy and her face flushed. Her clothing is just slightly off kilter. I smooth down my own hair, but I am certain it is too late. The knowing look in Errol's eyes tells me he has accurately deduced exactly what just happened.

"Carry on," he says cheerfully, his entire demeanor shifting radically. "Give me a report if anything develops." The glimmer in his eyes is a sure indication he plans on telling everyone that another mating ceremony is on the horizon.

When I glance over at Addison to gauge her reaction, I feel a stab of disappointment. She looks...uncomfortable, a flicker of uncertainty crossing her face.

But I try to suppress my reaction, try not to take offense. She is a private person. I am certain she simply wanted to reveal our connection in her own time.

But that disappointment still lingers despite myself as we get back to work. I do not like the suspicion that blooms inside me. What if...she never wanted to reveal our courtship?

Ever?

13

ADDISON

*T*he ore doesn't respond to the meteorite glass. I've run through every possible way I can think of to make it work. Even some ways I never thought were possible. The shields and the old tech seem completely hopeless and out of reach, even more so now after that surprise hope. I pinch the bridge of my nose, closing my eyes for a moment as I think.

Maybe I need to take a break from this and work on something else. The invaders' ship maybe—it's no longer a side project. We need the low-tech cart that it came with, but so far, nothing we've tried has succeeded in unlocking it.

I certainly can't read the directions. The writs still elude me, another point of frustration, especially since cracking them could have really helped me figure out how to open the cart.

As I turn to the problem of the cart, I feel a deep sense of disappointment—in myself. I feel like I've failed and now I'm giving up, even though I tell myself I'm just switching gears for the moment.

It puts me in a terrible, ugly mood that I just can't seem to shake by falling into the new problem. Focusing on work usually helps. But not this time.

"I brought lunch for you, Addison," Melchior murmurs when he comes into the lab not much later. "It is a good time to take a break."

"Can't you see I'm working, Melchior?" I snap, not looking up. "Your interruptions aren't exactly helpful."

As soon as I say the words and feel the shift in the air, I immediately regret them.

When I look up at Melchior's face, I can see the hurt and confusion in his expression and feel even more terrible.

"Sorry," I quickly say. "Thank you for the food. I just...I need to focus, okay?"

He nods stiffly, his expression smoothing out. Not in a good way. More like he's putting on a mask to cover up.

"Of course," he murmurs, setting the food down near me and stepping away. "I shall not disturb you again."

Oh no. The comment really stung. And I don't think my apology was enough to smooth things over.

He settles into work alongside me, but the unfamiliar tension between us is...not great, and he doesn't speak to me like he usually does while we're in the lab. He's silent. Coldly so. Working in that chill is extremely uncomfortable.

I glance at his stone face from time to time, coming up with and discarding possible ways to break it. I hate the silent treatment. But I also know I was out of line.

I slide on a mitt and pick up one of the pieces of vanadium while I rack my brain for the best way to break the ice, maybe to apologize again.

Melchior is wonderful. Sweet, caring, always right there when I need him. I feel like a complete ass for being mean, for taking out my frustration on him when he was trying to be his usual thoughtful self. I'm so bad at this...whatever this is between us. But I'm worse at staying in this uncomfortable silence with him angry at me, so I finally decide just to dive right in.

Fuck it.

"Melchior, I—" I turn towards him with the ore in my hand, not knowing exactly what I'm going to say, but deciding anything is better than nothing.

But I shut my mouth abruptly as an odd click echoes in the lab.

And the cart, shut tight as a drum all this time while it sat next to us, just...opens.

I stare at it, totally flummoxed.

"What the..." I gasp, looking down at the ore in my hand. Was it as easy as waving the stupid ore at it? Really? But that can't be right. I've had the ore near it for a while now.

I shake my head, excitement bubbling up inside me as I get closer to the open cart. Who cares how it happened! There's time to figure out how I did it later. Right now, I just want to celebrate the fact that something actually went right in here for once! Maybe not through any real intent on my part, but I'll take anything at this point.

I turn back to Melchior to revel in the moment with him, but then I pause. He's already leaving the lab.

"I'll report the progress to Errol," he throws back at me over his shoulder. And then he's gone.

What? I stare at the empty door. The empty lab.

I try to hold on to that feeling of excitement, of accomplishment and success, but my heart can't hold on to it. All of that joy just leaks right back out of me. I immediately deflate, because Melchior isn't there to enjoy this moment with me.

I turn away, covering my face with my hands. I didn't mean to snap at him. He didn't deserve it at all.

A flash of memory hits me, of my mother snapping at me for anything and everything, her bitterness seeping into all aspects of life. I know I tend to do the same. Despite my best intentions, I've learned bad habits from her that I can't always shake. Including the snapping, a defensive technique that isn't at all productive. Just hurtful.

I sit down on the stool, propping my elbows on the table to brace my head.

I went through a period where I was basically an emotional porcupine. My defenses were always up, a way to keep everyone at arm's length. So they couldn't hurt me. But I've kept a fairly tight lid on that tendency for years, worked hard so I could build relationships.

Up until now.

When it really counts.

"Ugh!"

I lay my head down on the cool table, barely resisting the urge to bang it on the surface repeatedly. This sucks. This really, really sucks.

Damn it.

14

MELCHIOR

"*T*hat is wonderful news!" Errol exclaims, genuinely excited.

"Yes, it is," I agree in a much more reserved manner.

Errol gives me a slightly odd look at my response. Perhaps I am not showing the same level of excitement at the news that the invaders' cart is now open, but I cannot pretend that everything is fine. It is the best I can do.

"Well, I shall go inform Rosalind and Visidion of this newest development," he announces after a brief, awkward pause. "Give my congratulations to Addison!"

I murmur my agreement, watching him hurry out to spread the news.

With no other reason to delay my return to the lab and Addison, I turn to walk back. Slowly. The truth is, despite my hurt feelings at the way Addison snapped at me, I am actually quite proud of her. I have always believed hard work and perseverance are key to accomplishing most things in life and Addison is a prime example of that. But I simply cannot display that emotion, not yet. Not when I keep replaying how dismissive she was towards me, how condescending. As if I do not know that she needs to focus, that what she is doing is important! Does she believe I am stupid?

I suppress another growl at the thought, indignant that she would even imply such a thing. Especially when all I was trying to do was help her, bring her food so she would not have to waste time and energy leaving the lab to do so herself! Even thinking about it raises my ire once more.

I stop before I enter the lab, taking a deep breath and deliberately erasing the emotion off of my face before I step inside. I do not want her to know how much she can erode my control by doing something like this, do not want to give her more power than she already has over me.

When I enter, I do not go to Addison first, ask her if she needs help or if she has made any additional progress on her projects as I usually do. No, I go directly to work myself without acknowledging her.

If she does not want interruptions, does not want my help, then fine. I will not give it to her. Even as I do this, a small part of me knows that my actions are somewhat petty, but I do not stray from the path. Perhaps later I will be more centered, more able to behave reasonably, but this is the best I can do for now.

I can feel Addison glance at me and then look away, uncomfortable with my mostly silent manner. I know she does not know how to respond to me while I am behaving this way. She has only ever interacted with the softest part of me. The part of me that only wants to care for her, only wants her to be comfortable at all times, wants to speak to her despite my hurt feelings, wants this tension between us to dissipate. But I stay strong.

She will have to issue an apology, a real and sincere one, not that automatic one she muttered out of reflex when she realized she had offended me. A verbal apology that I feel is appropriate and sufficient.

I refuse to mirror some of the relationships she had on the ship, refuse to allow us to start on that foot.

The time she always seems to stop speaking of when thoughts of her mother cause her to tense up.

She obviously did not have the type of relationship with her parent that she should have had, and I know that can leave scars, invisible ones that often only come out during times of stress.

But I deserve her effort, deserve her trying to be better than her past. I am more than simply a "lover" as I have heard human females call males they only have sexual relations with. I am her friend, and I demand better, demand what I know she can give.

Even as I think that, I cannot ignore her completely. As I continue to work, I keep a discreet eye on her. It is clear that she is having trouble focusing because of the chill currently between us. She keeps glancing at me and then looking away, a thoughtful frown on her face.

I can almost feel her processing her thoughts. She may not realize it yet, but I know part of the reason she has been so irritable is that Errol has deduced what is going on between us, and she does not like the exposure. She does not like that we would be linked so publicly.

And I think I know why. There is a reason why she dresses so conservatively, why she likes to minimize her beauty as much as she can while other females attempt to enhance their own.

She loves the lab, loves her work.

And she wants to be taken seriously. So she presents herself in what she considers a serious manner. Which makes no sense to me. What about physical beauty or femininity would make anyone think less of her? One would have to be a complete idiot to disregard her intelligence, her hard work and dedication simply because of her outward presentation.

However, I am quite certain I am on the correct track with my thoughts.

Unfortunately for me, I think this same incorrect idea she has about her outward physical appearance also extends to any relationships. Specifically, any relationship with a male, which in this case, is me. She fears that mating me would mean that she would no longer be taken seriously, that nobody would recognize her for her own merit.

Another ridiculous thought!

I do not know why she is so insecure that she would fear such a thing when she is obviously an integral part of the tech team here in the city. And I am put off by it. I do not like her thinking of me as a burden, a liability that she must keep hidden. Good enough to be with, but only under the cover of darkness where nobody can see. Where nobody can judge her.

I press my lips together in frustration, putting down my own tools to take a deep breath so I do not accidentally damage the mechanical components in front of me.

I glance over at Addison, catching her looking at me. She turns her head quickly away, her cheeks flushing in embarrassment.

My heart softens, just as it always does in her presence. Even while I am angry with her, frustrated at her behavior, I feel the urge be compassionate—to attempt to understand her reasoning, the past that created the person she is today.

It is difficult to know exactly what I should do. This...our relationship...is difficult.

Human ways are not Zmaj ways, even though the blending of our people has caused sure and lasting changes to this portion of Tajss, shifting the cultural and social dynamics in a unique way. But that blending does not mean we have an instant and perfect understanding of each other.

She glances at me once more, looking away again when

she realizes I am still focused on her. I want to go to her. Want to comfort her and tell her everything will be fine. But I harden my resolve and look away.

No. I cannot do that. I need to establish this boundary now to ensure our relationship is stronger in the future. I cannot give in to my softer side, no matter how strong the temptation.

She owes me a proper apology. So I continue to work quietly, though I do not get much of significance done. It is difficult to focus with such emotional turmoil taking place inside.

I breathe a silent sigh of relief when Rosalind finally arrives with Visidion and Errol in her wake. Anything to distract from this tension.

Addison stands to greet them, but her eyes tend to want to stay on Rosalind.

"The cart is open?" Rosalind asks, stepping over to the piece of machinery without waiting for an answer. "Bravo, Addison. Bravo."

Addison beams, the admiration she holds for the other woman clear in her expression, in the way she angles her body to towards the other woman.

"Well, I'm not exactly sure yet how I did it, but..."

As she speaks, I stare. This does not make any kind of sense to me. If she holds the Lady General Rosalind in such high regard, how can she have misgivings toward our mating?

Rosalind and Visidion's mating is no secret. In fact, it is often assumed that where one may find Rosalind, one may also find Visidion. It has not affected her authority at all. In fact, Visidion has only enhanced how seriously everyone responds to Rosalind. With such a strong Zmaj Tribe Commander supporting her, how could anyone with a brain not view her as an even more formidable power? And if

Rosalind can mate with one of us and maintain her status, why does Addison think she cannot? Why would she put this distance between us, display unwarranted aggression to achieve it? It is maddening.

"You simply waved the ore over the cart and it opened?" Errol asks, skeptical.

Addison nods.

"Yes. Though I don't know if that was all it is because there's been ore around the cart for a while now." She shrugs. "I'm going to have to do some more experimentation to pin things down."

"Hmm. Do think perhaps this is why the invaders want the vanadium?" Visidion asks, staring at the cart.

"You mean because it seems able to unlock compartments and locks on their ship?" Addison clarifies, nodding slowly. "That makes sense. Seems like even if the ore isn't integral to their tech, it would be damn inconvenient for us to be able to just wave the ore and unlock their stuff without even an 'Open Sesame' needed."

"'Open Sesame'?" Errol repeats with a frown.

"Just a generic term used to stand in for a password," Rosalind murmurs. "I think Addison is right—I certainly wouldn't want my enemies to have keys to any of our equipment. And taking the keys is immensely more efficient than attempting to change all of their tech, all of their ships and vehicles so they don't respond to the ore. If that's even possible for them to do."

We all murmur our agreement with that statement. I would certainly try to secure such keys if at all possible.

"We need to guard the mining settlement carefully," Rosalind continues, her gaze shifting to the box full of the vanadium. "Even if we don't figure out a way for the ore to work for our shields or our technology...it's still a valuable commodity." She looks over at Addison. "And I'm still not convinced that you guys won't figure out how to make it work for us too."

Addison flushes at the vote of confidence.

"I can't guarantee results, but I'm down to keep trying."

I look away, feeling an uncharacteristic resentment bubble to the surface. If only Addison were so invested in us.

15

ADDISON

I finally give up on trying to get more sleep around dawn. Throwing off even the thin covers I prefer in the perpetual heat here, I flop onto my back.

I'm supposed to travel to the Tribe today so I can try out an idea I have on the machine that powers the shield there. Normally, I know I'd be excited at the prospect of something like this, of being able to test out a theory, work out the kinks on site. I do like a challenge, even with the frustration with all of the projects I've been working on.

But rather than looking forward to it, even despite the pressure to succeed, I find myself almost dreading the journey. A first for me, and it's no mystery why. Worse, I'm feeling this way because of something I did. I feel the urge to slap myself.

Melchior is still clearly angry at me, which would be bad enough. But what's really terrible is I know he's also hurt under that cold demeanor. I'm so not good at this emotional stuff!

"Ugh!"

I flip onto my stomach and smash my face into the pillow

as I contemplate the hard truth of this particular shortcoming. I know how it developed, but knowing the problem and fixing it are two very different things. On the ship, there was always this expectation of maintaining a certain...unfeeling perfection in the scientific teams. Something even the other high-level professionals in other fields strived to achieve, like a badge of honor.

Not because we were all cold as people, but because doing our jobs in the most effective manner meant we needed to put emotions aside. Put all biases we had aside, really. They aren't conducive to good work.

But compartmentalizing my emotional self like that day in and day out...I guess I didn't realize exactly how much of a toll that took on me. Combined with the unhealthy habits and traits I acquired from my mother...yeah. Really not a great combination.

I'm just not used to having to deal with my emotions and work at the same time, but with Melchior right there in the lab with me, that's just going to come up. Naively, I didn't even consider that possibility, though I guess I should have. I mean, I've been mooning over him for some time now, and that's affected my work somewhat too, right? Maybe not quite to this extent, but it was definitely a unique experience for me to be distracted by a man I was attracted to. It had never come up before. I always kept the two deliberately separate.

To make matters worse, I know I've managed to keep a tight lid on my mother's more unsavory traits, but that lid blew right off with Melchior. Like he just short circuited those defenses without even trying. Just with his presence alone.

I flip over again, taking a deep breath. I guess...I've never felt quite this intensely about someone before. And I just don't know how to handle it. I know it's also just triggering a whole bunch of insecurities in me, activating my abandonment issues in a big way. Maybe part of the problem is...that I don't even know if we'll last, that he'll even stay with me in the long run.

Driving him away before he can leave on his own gives me that control that I so need in my life after the chaos of my childhood. The thing is, that analysis is all well and good, but it's no excuse for treating him badly. Not when he's been nothing but good to me.

I should apologize for pushing him away. A real apology, not that quick one I gave right after I took out my frustration on him.

What I really want to do is stay in bed all day. But I don't. I rub at my eyes and sit up. I can't lay in bed any longer. I have to get ready and head out to meet Melchior for the trip. I'm sure being late won't help his mood.

Sliding my legs off the bed and bracing my feet on the floor, I try to gear up for the journey.

I can do this—I will get through this. I keep repeating that in my head while I get ready. All the way up until I walk out to the edge of the city, where Melchior is waiting for me. As soon as I see his cold face, his guarded gaze, I lose the Words of Affirmation.

It really hurts when he looks at me like that. I've only ever seen him watch me with soft eyes, with admiration and desire. I didn't even realize I came to expect it, like the bright sunlight here. This shift makes me feel like something you'd scrape off the bottom of your shoe.

"Are you ready?" he greets me, not bothering with pleasantries. He's been keeping communication to a minimum. Just the facts, ma'am. I feel like this would be better if he just tore into me and got it over with. But I guess that isn't in his personality.

I just nod, matching his verbal efficiency. "Yes."

I step towards him a little hesitantly, somewhat afraid for the first time that he may not want me to touch him, even if it is only for the purposes of faster traveling.

I breathe a silent sigh of relief when he doesn't step away. But the business-like way he wraps his arm around my waist is different than before. How can the same gesture, the same movement, feel so completely off? I don't know, but I can feel it. Like he's touching me only as much as he needs to and no more. It's not nearly as comforting.

Spreading his wings, he takes off with me attached to him. But I may as well be a pack of supplies strapped to his body. That's how distant he feels even though his side is pressed up against me. It's actually kind of impressive how he gets his point across while still holding me.

We stop once, halfway through the journey, taking cover in the shade of a rock formation and eating.

"Would you like more of the jerky?" I ask, holding out a piece. As peace offerings go, it isn't much, but I don't know what else to do.

"No, thank you," he responds immediately, not even turning to look at me. With a pang, I realize he hasn't faced me during the entire trip. The only time we've made eye contact today is when I first met him at the edge of the city. I thought maybe a break would be a good time for me to broach the elephant in the room—or maybe it would be more appropriate to call it the guster in the desert. Whatever.

But the freezer burn I'm getting just from being near him makes me put it off. Cowardly, maybe. But if things go wrong, we'll still have half the journey to go with me holding on to him like a monkey. I can't handle things being even more uncomfortable than they are now, especially if I can't move away to lick my wounds afterwards.

Okay, fine. I'll approach him about this once we're at the

Tribe. And either or both of us can get some space if we need it.

He must be keeping an eye on me even if he's not looking at me directly, because as soon as I'm done eating, he stands.

"Come. I do not want to waste any time unnecessarily."

I nod at the terse words, adjusting my own pack and stepping towards him. I can't help but reflect on our previous journey to the Tribe as he wraps his arm around me again. I almost feel like I'm with a different person altogether. For the first time, I understand how silence can be deafening.

At least we don't encounter any of Tajss' beasts on the way there. I'm willing to grasp at any silver lining at this point. I feel relief when we see the distinctive wall come into sight. At least this particular low-grade torture will be over. But as soon as we make it to the Tribe's cave system, Melchior steps away.

"I need to speak with someone."

Not waiting for any kind of response, he promptly disappears. Ouch. Though I guess I am a little relieved to escape the silent treatment and the cold shoulder.

"Hey, Addison!" Fallon calls out, pausing with a basket full of produce. "What are you doing here?"

"Hey, Fallon. I needed to test out a theory with the machine that powers the shield here," I explain, waving vaguely in its direction.

"Ah." She adjusts her basket as she steps away. "That's great! Good luck—I know all of us will feel a lot better if we can get a permanent fix for that thing."

"Thanks," I murmur, watching her leave.

At least someone appreciates me right now. Shaking my head at myself, I head directly over to the machine. At least I can be productive.

Unstrapping my pack and taking out the tools I brought with me, I hunker down. As I work, I also kick myself. I should have apologized during the trip, despite how awkward it was.

At least we had a good amount of privacy out there. I feel like anywhere we go here, someone could hear us through no fault of their own. It's not like there are real doors to block out sounds, just curtains for visual privacy. It's not like I can talk to him anyway, if he keeps running away as soon as he can. Maybe I should hold off and just do it on the trip back...

I mentally smack myself. I can't keep putting this off. If I continue to do that, this fight is going to become even harder to resolve. I know it isn't good to let things linger. A deeper rot can set in.

Okay, fine. I'm going to apologize to Melchior right after I finish with the machine. Even if that means dragging him away in front of everybody and finding a corner where we can talk.

I immediately feel better as the resolve washes through me. I have a plan and I'm going to stick to it. I need to fix this so I don't keep stressing about it and Melchior doesn't keep hurting and being angry.

I frown down at the machine. Hmm. Maybe if I—

"Attack! Weapons at the ready! We're under attack!"

Adrenaline shoots through me at the words, the familiarity of the situation making it feel surreal.

Again!?

Are they just waiting to make sure we're always here for everyone?

"Shit shit shit," I mutter to myself, immediately working to adjust the machine to ensure the shield is stable, at least for now. Any more tinkering is going to have to wait.

Grabbing the shock stick I have strapped to my back, I run over to the wall, joining the stream of Zmaj and women going in the same direction.

The staccato roars of the invaders are close.

Too close.

"They're past the shield!" one of the women screams, though I can't see who it is.

I feel a cold chill raise the hairs on the back of my neck. The shield was down briefly. But apparently at exactly the wrong time.

In the next moment, it doesn't matter.

A group of the cold-eyed aliens runs in past the wall, their mouths open as they scream their battle cries.

I turn on the shock stick, trying to remember everything Melchior taught me but coming up with a blank. A metallic taste fills my mouth as I fight down a sense of raw panic.

Odd details stand out. The particular texture on one of the invaders' cheek. The way that the light bounces off the thick ridge of another's. The sharp glint of claws at the end of their main three-fingered hands...

I flinch as Bashir leaps in front of me, taking down one of the invaders with a hard thrust of his lochaber.

Then it's like the dam has broken. Zmaj and invaders collide in a riot of sound and screams, but this time I'm not safely buffered, standing way in the back out of the action. There are too many, too close for the Zmaj to get all of them before they get to us.

I try to stay out of the way of the fights going on around me, the sheer confusion of being in the middle of the battle hitting me for the first time. There's so much sensory input that it's difficult to know where to look, friend and foe oddly blending together at odd times. For a few moments, I'm standing in the middle of chaos, in the eye of the storm going on around me.

And then I see a flash of that distinctive brown carapace. I turn towards it, bringing my shock stick up as I meet one of the invaders' black, flat eyes. I feel as though I'm moving through molasses, like I'm in a dream, though I know I must be moving fast.

My heart thuds in my ears, deep and slow. Thud. Thud. Thud.

I'm not going to be able to block or hit him in time. I see that immediately, even as I keep moving. He reaches out with those claws, the secondary arms flaring out at his sides, that mouth opening to display sharp teeth behind the hard tusks... I brace my legs and block one of those clawing hands with the shock stick, but the other digs into my side, sliding through my clothes and skin like they're paper.

I scream, twisting the shock stick to angle it towards the thing's neck, where the tough brown carapace doesn't protect its skin. Its claws swipe down my hip. I grit my teeth and brace myself.

I'm going to have to tear away from that hand before I can make contact with the shock stick. With a grunt, I jerk my hip back, the claws tearing out of me just as I force the prongs to make contact.

I stare into those dark, emotionless eyes as the shock hits him.

With a hard jolt, the invader jerks back, blown right off its feet by the force of the shock the stick delivers.

I step forward, something in me needing to make sure that I finish this, that he is dead. Blood drips down my side, a warm, disconcerting slide, and I find myself limping, but I still crouch down next to the still body and give it another jolt for good measure. The body convulses on the ground and I take a deep breath, pulling back.

Gone.

He's—it's? —gone.

I sit down on the ground right there next to the body.

The battle continues around me, the screams of pain, the sizzle of more shock sticks, the clang of sharpened metal poles as the women get involved, the grunts of effort, the sound of blades sinking into flesh.

I should get up.

I need to get up.

But I feel fuzzy, disconnected as I stare down at the body. Nothing feels quite real. Am I in shock?

A roar has me jerking my head up, finally. One of such rage and despair that I feel my own heart tremble with it, my stomach vibrates with the emotion behind it. A blur hits the body in front of me, the thing flopping as it gets thrown overhead and immediately speared with a lochaber.

Melchior turns to me, his face twisted in rage.

I freeze under those intense eyes. Not because of the anger or the intensity behind them. But because...it's like I'm looking at a completely different person.

Not the measured, in control, intelligent being that I know so well now. No, this is...someone else altogether. As I stare into those crazed eyes, I feel a shiver of fear go through me for an entirely different reason.

"Melchior..." I whisper, trying to stand.

Something flickers in his eyes. He steps forward towards me. A movement beyond his flared wings catches my eye before I can get to my feet.

"No!" I gasp. "Melchior, behind you!"

But he doesn't need my warning. Twisting hard, his powerful tail whipping out behind him, Melchior swings his lochaber hard and fast. And accurately. The leaping invader's head rolls right off its body mid-flight. But Melchior doesn't just let the body fall. Shifting to the side to let it fall to the ground, he slices off all of its arms on both sides with two hard slices.

Okay. That wasn't at all necessary. I swallow the bile that wants to rise, stepping back at the gruesome sight.

Melchior's wings rise and fall with his deep breaths as he

stands over the invader.

When he looks up, it isn't to turn back to me. With a snarl I can only hear, he crouches down and leaps up, propelling himself through the air, launching himself right into a knot of the invaders fighting off two women and one of the Zmaj.

Heart in my throat, I shake my head, expecting to see him mowed down by so many of the invaders around him. But I'm wrong. It is a massacre, yes. But the other way around.

I can't stop staring as Melchior moves so fast I can't properly even see what he's doing, his weapon shifting and turning, his body moving with a deadly grace. Blood sprays, and those odd staccato screams rend the air as heads roll, arms go flying, Melchior attacking with the precision of a surgeon.

The small group that had been trying to hold that group of invaders back actually retreats further at the frenzied attack. There's fear in their eyes. Fear for Melchior. When I turn back to him, he's already gone, leaving a trail of destruction in his wake.

I stare, my feet glued down to that spot as I watch. I can't look away. Why am I so certain something is terribly wrong?

"Addison." I flinch at a gentle hand on my arm. "You are wounded. Come."

I allow Bashir to swing me up into his arms and carry me out of the middle of the battle, back through the lines to a cave where there are other wounded.

"Shit, Addison," Fallon cries out when she sees me, helping me sit down. "Let's get you patched up."

I nod, looking down at my side and hip. Somehow, looking down at it, remembering that it's there, reactivates the searing pain.

"Is this the only place you're hurt?" she demands, tugging my clothes out of the way.

"I think so." I look around at the others sitting and bleeding. More than a few are women, though the wounds don't look too serious. "I can patch myself of," I protest as she comes to me with a wet rag. "It hurts, but I don't think they're actually that deep."

Fallon just gives me a look and gets to work cleaning the blood off, but when all's said and done, I'm actually right. That thing clawed me up well and good, but the wounds aren't so deep as to be of concern. A couple of sections do look like they might need some stitches, though.

"Let me just pour some of this disinfectant on them," she murmurs after a quick assessment. "And get the needle and thread."

I hiss as she literally upends a not-so-great smelling tincture bottle over the wounds.

"Shit, that stings," I gasp when she's done, my eyes watering.

"Better it sting now than you get an infection later," she points out, turning to grab some clean bandages and the dreaded needle and thread. "Here, I'm going to put on some numbing stuff before I start..."

Saturating a thin piece of cloth, she presses it over my wounds. I'm almost instantly numb, which I'm not at all complaining about. Thank you, drugs. Her hands are steady and competent as she gets to work. I can feel the tugging at my skin as she closes it up, which is really odd. I look away so I don't have to deal with the visual too. She's done in under ten minutes.

"All right, just let me bandage this and..."

But then Bashir arrives with someone else who needs help.

"Go," I order, taking the bandages. "I can do this part myself."

She hesitates, but then give me a quick all-encompassing glance. Apparently finding me in a good enough state, she stands up.

"All right—call if you need me."

I nod, already winding the cloth around myself. It isn't fun, but I manage to get it on tight enough that I think it'll stay. The wounds are starting to throb a little again, and they're definitely going to scar, but the bleeding has stopped.

When I stand, I realize I was limping because of a giant bruise on my thigh, not because of the wounds themselves. It must have happened during the same fight, but I didn't register it at all. Still, all in all, I got off pretty easy. Especially considering that my opponent is very, very dead.

Patched up as best as I can be, I steady myself against the stone. My only thought right then is about Melchior. Is he okay?

I can hear the sounds of the battle dying down and walk out of the cave to look. I just have a sick feeling in my gut. The way he looked when he tore into that invader...

I suppress a shiver, limping out to get a good view of the wall, of the battle. But when it comes into view again, I don't see more invaders streaming in. Actually, it looks like the battle is over and done, invaders' bodies littering the ground both past the wall and just inside.

I feel a trickle of relief flow through me, but less than I should be feeling after realizing the battle is over.

Where's Melchior?

And what are those sounds I thought were from the battle? I start to make my way closer to the wall when I hear an odd...growling? I look over to the side, near the wall, a section of it I couldn't see from my previous vantage point.

At first, I wonder why there's a group of Zmaj attacking one invader. I know they don't need that much manpower for just one of those things. But my step falters when I realize there is no invader in that tangled knot.

Melchior's crazed eyes meet mine as three of the other Zmaj finally manage to get him under control through brute force. My heart skips a beat. They start to drag him away while he continues to struggle against them, his face contorted with anger.

I take a step towards them, my heart in my throat as it starts beating again, fast and hard. What are they doing? But before I can get anywhere near them, Bashir steps in front of me, blocking my view with his body.

"What's going on?" I demand, trying to step past him. "What are you doing to Melchior?"

Bashir easily stops me from going around him, his hand gentle but firm on my upper arm.

"Melchior lost himself to his bijass," Bashir murmurs, glancing over his shoulder before looking back at me. "He must be contained for now. Not only for everyone else's safety, but for his own as well."

I stop trying to move around him.

"Bijass?" I repeat dumbly, everything I've heard of the state flickering through my mind.

"Yes," Bashir confirms, his eyes sympathetic. "Seeing you injured in the attack...he was unable to hold back the primal, brutal part of himself."

"Where are you taking him?" I ask through numb lips.

Bijass. I have a flash of Melchior's eyes as the three other Zmaj struggled to contain him. Three. That's how out of control he was. Is.

"We have a secured cave we used for...someone else in the past."

"Okay." Jail. They're jailing him. But after seeing him tear into the invaders like he did and after seeing how many of the others it took to restrain him...I understand the reasoning behind it. "Can I see him?"

Bashir's face softens, but he shakes his head slowly.

"I do not think it is a good idea for you to see him until he is more calm. The sight of you may only agitate him further in this state." Turning me around, he leads me to where the others are gathering to figure out the food situation. No matter what happens, we always have to eat. "You should eat something and rest while you wait. You will feel better."

I allow him to sit me down at a table, but I'm not thinking about food at all. How can I? I feel...empty. Completely at a loss. All I want is to have Melchior here, be able to hold him in my arms, tell him I'm sorry for everything. That I can't be without him.

For some reason, my brain goes to the first time I ever saw him. The first time I heard his voice. The kindness in his eyes, the way he always had time to help me, was always there when I needed him for anything. How he touched me when we were alone, the reverence in his eyes, in his hands...

The fierce way he protected me, even when he was lost to the bijass. I feel a stab of pain, of longing as the reel of memories plays in my mind.

What was I thinking? How could I have ever been anything but nice to him in return? Why did I ever doubt that I wanted him as close to me as possible? That he would be anything but a positive light in my life? Why didn't I give him the apology he deserved when I had a chance? How could I have been such an idiot?

I wish I could rewind things and just be...better. Better to him, and ultimately, myself. I scrub my hands over my face, so angry at myself.

I won't ever push him away again if only he...

I look back, back towards where they disappeared with him in tow.

"Come back to me, Melchior," I murmur, my throat closing with fear. "Come back."

How can I ever go back to the way my life was without him in it?

16

ADDISON

I straighten, arching my back with a groan. Staying bent over for long periods of time isn't exactly easy on my body, but it's kind of part of the job description. I sigh, looking down at the invaders' ship cart.

Yes, I was able to open it before, accident or no. But, unfortunately, that isn't the end of that. Opening the door is only the first step. I have to make it go.

Progress has been slow and frustrating, which I guess is to be expected at this point. No project so far has been easy— why should this one be any different?

I glare at it for a moment. Not that it cares. It's just sitting there, mocking me.

Okay, I might be losing it a little.

I glance around the empty lab and feel that now-familiar ache in my chest. The lab has always been my safe haven, the place I go where I can feel like I'm in control, where I know exactly what I'm doing. But Melchior quickly became an integral part of that haven, his familiar and comforting presence something I miss terribly.

Hell, what I wouldn't do to have him back here even cold

and pissed off at me, working silently in the corner. And isn't that telling?

Taking a deep breath, I look back at the cart. My newest source of frustration. I feel like I always have one at this point. At least the project is helping me get my mind off things somewhat while I wait to hear about Melchior's condition. As if on cue, my eyes prick with tears at the thought of him.

"God damn it," I mutter, tilting my head back to keep the tears from falling.

Okay, so the car isn't a foolproof distraction, but that's a lot to put on a piece of machinery anyway.

I find myself dreading the night more every day, when there's nothing to distract me from my inner monologue, nothing else to occupy my time, my mind. I've tried staying in the lab, but there comes a point where I'm so tired I'm afraid I'm going to do some damage to my progress if I keep going.

So, inevitably, I end up back in bed. Alone.

In that dark silence, my heart, my mind, they both reach out for Melchior, wanting, needing to feel his presence on the other end. Ever since we first became intimate with each other, I've felt this connection. This feeling, this sense of just...him. His presence, for a lack of a better term, in the background of my mind. I didn't even truly realize he was there until he vanished, until the bijass took him from me, ripped us apart. That must be the reason for the severing of that connection.

After the shock of the battle wore off while I was still with the Tribe, I realized I felt an odd hollowness. A nothingness where there should have been something, though I couldn't pinpoint what it was until later.

I drop my head, wrapping my arms around myself, warding off a chill that has nothing to do with the temperature of the room.

I've tried to reach out to him deliberately with my mind since that realization. Telepathically, I guess, though that word still makes me uncomfortable. But all I feel is a vast emptiness at the other end of that extension, a nothingness that makes me feel worse than before I tried. I feel like I keep worrying at an empty space where a tooth used to be.

Is he lost to me? I don't even want to consider it, but...

Staying with the Tribe day in and day out had not only started to drive me up the wall, it also meant important research and progress wasn't being made back here at the lab.

But maybe leaving had been a mistake. I should have stayed, should have fought for the right to see Melchior rather than going along with the ban like I did. I thought the other Zmaj knew better, had more experience. But do they?

And my thoughts have circled right back to where they always do, an endless cycle that I can't get out of.

I take a deep breath and try to re-focus. I'm not getting anywhere with this.

So I attempt to set aside my impatience with the waiting —for what feels like the thousandth time—and try to focus on the cart, on the problem in front of me that I can maybe actually do something about.

The cart isn't as impressive as Kate's rover, but it's still useful to have another vehicle on hand. Big enough to comfortably fit two or to cram in four, it should be sufficient when we need something to travel a longer distance. I don't know how fast it is, won't really know unless and until I can get the thing fully functional.

So that's what I work on. I don't need to be able to conquer every bell and whistle that comes with the thing, I just need to figure out how to get it running. I throw myself into the work, trying one thing after another, tweaking and adjusting until I have to shake out my hands before I step back.

I stare at it.

I think I may have done it.

It should be fully functional.

I lift the door up on the side and sit down in the bench seat up front.

From what I can gather, there isn't so much a driver's seat as there is a driver's section up front here.

Fiddling with the controls, I hold my breath.

There aren't any foot pedals, just multiple levers and buttons.

I guess that makes sense when you have six arms...

Taking hold of the largest one, I say a quick prayer and slowly ease it forward.

It might not respond right away. There might be—

"Shit!"

I let go as I shoot forward three yards almost instantly. A shot of adrenaline flows through me as I quickly find the brake through a very brief trial and error situation.

It stops just a foot from the wall. I stare at flat surface, letting out a huff of breath.

That was way too close.

It would have been really embarrassing if I managed to destroy the lab like that. I'd never live it down.

I climb out of the cart on slightly shaky legs, staring at the cart in its new position. I look around for good measure, but I've been alone in here for hours. Nobody was here to witness my less-than-smart mistake.

Moving back, I sit down on one of the stools nearby and stare at the cart. It's ready to go, at least for a test drive.

I glance at the clock. Early afternoon. I should really go find Rosalind and share the good news. I know she'll be happy to hear it. But I find myself hesitating as I look back at the vehicle.

I still haven't gotten any news about Melchior, not even a progress update. It's all I can think about.

I stare at the cart some more, biting my lip.

What I'm thinking is stupid. Stupid, crazy, and irresponsible.

I crack my knuckles, still not getting up to go find the Lady General. The cart isn't mine. I can't just take it on what Rosalind would consider a superfluous and dangerous trip. I really shouldn't even be considering it. It's a clear indication that I've fully and completely gone off the deep end.

Aaaand, I'm still sitting on the stool. Not making any move to go find Rosalind.

You know what? I'm tired of always being responsible.

Fuck it.

I jump to my feet and hurry over to the large double doors that stay closed for the most part. We only open them when we have a large piece of equipment to run into or out of the lab. They open into a small side street that doesn't have much foot traffic, which makes it really convenient for bringing in all manner of things.

And which will be very convenient now for me to...borrow the cart to travel to the Tribe and Melchior. It's reckless. But I find I just don't care anymore.

I open one of the doors to stick my head out to do a quick recon of the immediate area.

Empty.

Most people in the city are probably eating right now. And if I leave immediately, I may be able to reach the Tribe before night falls.

Assuming nothing goes wrong. Like a meteor shower, or a zemlja attack, or—

Okay, stop.

My mind is already made up. There's no point in scaring myself more about exactly how great of an undertaking it is to travel across the desert alone, even in the relative safety of a vehicle.

Flinging both doors open I hurry back to the vehicle to hop in, but then stop myself. I need supplies. Luckily, I have some food and water waiting in the wings anyway. If I'm in the middle of something, I don't particularly like to leave the lab. The snacks and water should be enough to tide me over for the trip. And I don't want to risk going out to get anything more and running into somebody. They might pick up on my shadiness. I feel like my intentions are written all over my face right now.

I load up the cart and then get inside, pressing the button that closes the door. As soon as it lowers and locks into place, I grip the lever and move the cart forward.

I'm more careful this time, using only the gentlest pressure to ease it out of the lab. I don't want to ram the thing into a building. That'll be a quick goodbye to any kind of attempt at stealth.

Once outside, I stop it and slide out to close the doors behind me. If anyone goes into the lab, they'll immediately notice the cart is gone. That's not something I can hide.

But there's no reason to clue people in quicker by leaving the doors wide open. If they find out too soon, they'll try to stop me, both for my own safety and for the cart itself. It's a valuable resource, so I would understand, but I still don't want it to happen.

I take a circuitous route out of the city, avoiding the areas and streets that are used the most. My hand grips the lever nervously while I drive, knowing just one pair of eyes might be enough to ruin my plan. Well, if you can even call this half-assed road trip a plan. Maybe I should call it my spiral into mental illness.

I avoid the main entrance and exit point—too many eyes. After bringing the vehicle to a slow stop at the edge of the city, I scan the desert just outside. There are Zmaj on patrol around the city, making sure we aren't taken unawares by invaders or even just the dangerous fauna of Tajss.

I don't want to accidentally run right into someone...

There. I can't make out who it is specifically, but the familiar glint of sunlight off scales and the distinctive shape of wings and tail make the Zmaj warrior easy to identify. I wait until he's out of sight. He might still see me, or someone else might, but it's the best I can do.

I'm hoping if anyone does see me, they'll just assume I'm taking the cart on a sanctioned test run. The fact that I've never done anything crazy might work in my favor.

Okay.

Here I go.

Swallowing dryly, I carefully drive out onto the desert, the change of the ground underneath me clearly apparent.

The sand slows down the vehicle slightly, but it's built for all terrain, so it still works smoothly. It would be truly idiotic if the invaders brought anything to Tajss that couldn't be driven on sand.

My instinct is to go slowly, so I can watch out for any more Zmaj on patrol—but I don't.

I have a narrow window here where I just might be able to get out of the city and its surrounding area without being stopped. Hesitating now could be my downfall.

I move quickly, hoping the fact that I'm leaving will be helpful. After all, the patrols are on the lookout for attacks, not for people leaving the city. We're not in a prison.

I almost hold my breath as I pass the area where I saw the Zmaj pass through. I don't know how much farther I have to be to be completely out of sight. I'm hoping the ripple of the sand, the up and down dip of the dunes, will help hide me.

I drive for a good ten minutes before my shoulders finally relax somewhat and I let out a sigh of relief. I think I'm out of the danger zone. Now all I have to do is travel through the desert without being attacked, getting lost, or having the newly fixed vehicle die on me.

Piece of cake.

I've never been more aware of my surroundings as I drive in what I'm pretty sure is the right direction. I was careful to make a note of the landmarks that I should pass the last time Melchior took me to the Tribe, just in case. I figured it was good to have that knowledge, though I never expected to have to use it so soon. But I'm glad I paid attention.

"Close to the right direction" could really screw you out here. I could easily miss the Tribe's cave system altogether if I'm not careful, end up at a point miles away because I started just slightly off. When I see the first cluster of rocks I'm on the lookout for, I relax a little more. Okay, at least I'm on the right path. I wasn't entirely sure before.

There's a sameness to the red roll of sand out here that is really disconcerting. I feel it particularly acutely now that I'm completely alone. Really alone.

Actually, I don't think I've ever been this far away from all people before. Not on the ship, in the tunnels, or now in the city or with the Tribe. Huh. It doesn't help that there isn't a whole lot to break the silence.

I try not to think about that as I continue to drive, focusing on keeping a watch all around the vehicle. But despite my anxiety and fear, I find the sameness of the passing landscape slowly lulling me into an almost hypnotic state.

Almost like highway hypnosis, a term I encountered multiple times in the archives of the past on the ship. Come to think of it, I would really welcome a highway, a clear path to indicate where I'm going instead of the vastness of the desert all around me. I stir somewhat as I pass a familiar ridge, mentally checking it off the list. I missed a particular oasis on the way due to that trance like state, but I'm still quite confident of my direction.

I try to stay more aware after that, but I find myself settling back into that odd state. It's like my mind simply can't stay hyper aware while I'm driving through so much that looks the same. So when a flash of movement hits the corner of my eye, it takes me a moment to respond.

What was that?

Heart skipping a beat, I turn to look. I don't see anything immediately and start to wonder if there really was anything in the first place, or if my mind has started to play tricks on me out here...

There!

I squint my eyes, staring at that gap between dunes ahead of me.

What is that...?

I see another flicker, but this time I'm closer and I can actually make out shapes.

My blood chills as I realize exactly what it is I'm seeing. The hulking mounds and twitching tail are unmistakable. Heart in my throat, I have to make a quick decision.

Turn around, stop, or keep going with a route adjustment?

If I keep moving, it might draw attention to me, and I am not at all confident that this thing can outrun a pack of guster. That's not what it's made for, at a guess.

Feeling a fresh layer of sweat break out over my already-hot body, I slowly bring the cart to a stop. There's nowhere to take cover, nothing but sand as far as the eye can see. My breathing sounds loud in the confines of the cart as I wait.

This feels like the worst-case scenario for traveling

through the desert on my own. I don't know why I didn't expect it. Things going wrong seems to be the norm.

My breath catches as the first one appears from behind the dune to my left and ahead of me. I stopped with some distance between us, but it isn't like I'm not in full view. I feel painfully exposed, even in sitting in the cart, but maybe if I don't move they won't look over.

It's the hope I cling to as another one follows the first into view.

And then another.

And another.

Four total.

I don't know if it's the same group from last time. I'm not exactly skilled at telling guster apart. All I know is that they look pretty damned big right now as they cross in front of me.

Come on, keep going. Nothing to see here. The mounds of their back shift and sway as they continue to walk, a leisurely stroll, their wide webbed feet keeping them above the sand despite their mass.

I've never actually seen them moving so slowly. Then again, I've only seen them in attack mode.

My heart is beating so hard and fast while I watch that I'm surprised they can't hear it, that they aren't running right over to me. I have no illusions about what will happen if they do turn their attention to me. The cart is fine for travel, but there's no way I'll be able to outrun four of them from this distance and no way the cart will keep me safe with their concerted effort.

It will be a death sentence.

Okay, maybe I shouldn't be focusing so hard on that.

The first one disappears from view, behind another dune to the right, without so much as a glance over. Then the second, its tail whipping behind it as it follows.

But the third hesitates. I don't know why it turns its head to look over in my direction. I haven't moved at all. But it looks over, opening its mouth slightly, displaying those glistening, sharp teeth. That horrifying howl-hiss escapes its mouth, muffled only slightly by the cart.

I swallow, resisting the urge to jam the vehicle into reverse and run.

I can't act rashly.

It hasn't made a move towards me yet, and running usually activates the hunting instinct, making the predator want to chase. As much as I want to run, it might spell my death sentence.

So I white knuckle the seat under me and stay in place, a drop of cold sweat sliding down my spine as I watch. I keep breathing slow and even, shallow. I can't move, can't draw attention...

Why did I think coming out here alone was a good idea?

The fourth guster bumps its head into the one in front and that great head whips about, that howl hiss now directed at its counterpart.

The fourth just hisses back and walks past without a by-your-leave, clearly unimpressed with the display. I hold my breath as the third continues on, its gaze now on the other guster rather than me.

Within a few more seconds they're all out of sight.

But I stay frozen, only moving my eyes to look around me, straining to catch any hint of movement.

I stay like that for five minutes.

Then ten.

At fifteen, I finally take a deep breath, slumping in my seat, wiping at my sweaty face.

I'm all right.

I'm okay.

I grab some water and take small sips. The mundane act helps.

I take a few deep breaths before starting the cart once more and easing forward, keeping an eye out in case the pack decides to circle back around. When I don't immediately see them, I push the cart as fast as it can go.

At this point, I just want to get to the Tribe as fast as possible. I don't know if I could handle it if something else goes wrong. It takes some time before I'm not jumping at every little thing. Thankfully, the rest of the trip is uneventful.

When I see the sunlight glinting off the wall in front of the Tribe's cave system, I breathe a sigh of relief.

"Thank God," I say to myself, taking the cart all the way down to the edge.

Before anyone can raise an alarm about an unknown vehicle, I step out of the cart and hurry in past the wall. I see one of the Zmaj on patrol continue after a brief hesitation. If they ask me questions, I'll have to answer.

But I only have one person on my mind right now, and I don't want to linger long enough for someone to stop me. I don't doubt someone will if they realize I'm going to see Melchior.

I don't know exactly where they're holding him, but I do know the general direction they took him in. So that's where I go, keeping my head down and hurrying.

Nobody's going to stop me, not after I trekked across the whole freaking desert by myself. I dare anyone to try, honestly. I am so not in the mood.

Luckily, it doesn't actually take me very long to find where he's being held.

When I do, I feel my stomach drop a little. There are metal bars blocking the entrance to his cave. I know he needs to be restrained, but seeing him in a cage like this...

My eyes shift to the figure inside the dim interior. His hair is a mess, his hands clenched into fists as he prowls around the small space, complete with a cot and a small table and chair. I can feel the intensity of his energy, the frustration.

The rage.

I've seen footage of lions and tigers in cages, all that strength and energy trapped. That's exactly what this reminds me of. It doesn't feel right, even if they think it's necessary.

I stay silent, just watching him for a moment. Just seeing him is like a soothing balm to the soul. I feel like my everything is in there, trapped under a wall of that seething anger that I can't fully understand, not at the level he seems to be feeling it at anyway.

I don't say anything as I watch, not really expecting a reaction if he is as far gone as they say. I don't know what I expect, really. He hasn't responded to any of my telepathic attempts to reach out to him. Maybe he won't respond to me here now either.

The thought sends a fresh stab of fear and loss through me.

Have I left it too long? Am I too late?

But even as the edge of that panic fades slightly, I see Melchior's shoulders tense, the hard muscle cut. He's leaner than he was even from just these few days. Is he refusing to eat?

He turns around fast, his tail whipping out behind him, his wings flaring slightly. The unexpected swiftness of the movement startles me, but I resist the urge to step back in response.

He's behind bars.

He can't hurt me.

I don't want him to see me afraid of him, even in this state.

His eyes, those eyes that haunt me in my dreams these days, they find my own and lock on.

Outwardly, nothing happens.

But I feel the energy in that cell shift, morph into something else. Something...softer.

He takes a step towards me but doesn't close the entire distance. Almost like...he's afraid to?

I step forward to wrap my hands around the cold metal of the bars, holding his eyes, hope fluttering in my chest.

I can see Melchior in them. Can see his personality seeping back into that verdant green.

I want nothing more than to run in there, to take him into my arms, to pepper his face with kisses, but all I can give him right then are words.

I give him the ones that truly matter, the ones that might pierce through the last bit of that barrier that I can feel lingering.

"I am yours, Melchior. All yours." I grip the bars tighter as his eyes sharpen. "All yours...and waiting."

17

MELCHIOR

I hear her voice as though from a great distance, ebbing and flowing like waves lapping at the sand.

I close my eyes, focusing on the lovely, soothing sound of it.

But I know it cannot be real. Just as the vision of her outside the cold bars was not true. I know it cannot be.

She does not trust me. Has not fully accepted me as hers. Why would she be here now?

I continue to pace around the small cage they have secured me in, knowing when to turn and when to adjust my wings without thinking or looking.

I have been in here for...some time. How much time I am not clear on.

I shake my head, covering my ears with my palms as I continue to hear that familiar, impossible voice. It hurts to hear it when I know it is not real. When I know she is not here. Why won't it go away? Growling to myself, I continue to pace around the cage, thoughts coming in and leaving, too fast for me to grasp. They are slippery things indeed. Though perhaps not quite as difficult to corral as they were...

The entire time, her voice does not stop. I frown as I realize it isn't the same everywhere in the small cave I've been confined to. The next time I go around, I slow near the bars.

Yes. Her voice is stronger here. I fight through the maze of my mind, through the half-formed thoughts, struggling to understand the words that voice is forming.

Addison's voice.

"...you have to release him! He isn't dangerous anymore!"

"I understand your desire to do so." A rumbling male voice. A familiar one...Drosdan. Drosdan's voice. "But we simply cannot be sure that he is fully in control yet. It is not safe to release him too early if he is still lost to the bijass."

The bijass.

I was...lost to the bijass. Yes, that makes sense. I cannot think, cannot trust what I see or hear because I was lost to that dark, primitive part of my mind.

But the fact that I am even now hearing these words and understanding them is proof the bijass is fading.

"I'm telling you he isn't lost to the bijass anymore!" Her tone is irritated now, even more demanding. "Why aren't you listening?"

A laugh forms in my chest as I imagine her staring down the much larger male. She sounds fierce indeed, a force to be reckoned with. That is my female...

I still at that thought.

No.

I shake my head, agitated. I cannot call her my female. She has not fully given herself to me the way I need, the way I crave.

I have been waiting, waiting too long for her. For all of her.

"Addison, I simply cannot—"

"He's my mate, Drosdan," she responds in a low voice.

Her matehood right. She is asserting her matehood right.

Silence falls in the wake of that pronouncement. It is clear, decisive. Unmistakable.

As if my mind was waiting for just that moment, I feel a door within burst open. And a wave suffused with Addison washes over me.

I feel her.

Her struggle to fight back tears. Her heart, fully open to me. Her fear of losing me. The emotions are strong, undeniable. Addison's emotions.

I feel...full.

Joy bubbles up inside me, pushing the darkness back even more. This, this is what I needed, what I wanted. What I have dreamed of. But I do not want her to feel this way. I want to heal every inch of doubt she has, leave nothing dark within her.

I can feel her fear that I will leave. A foolish fear indeed. I will never leave her. Ever. She is everything I have ever wanted, ever needed.

And now she is mine.

I will never let my treasure go.

Lost in the wonder of this new connection, I do not realize Drosdan is at the door until I hear the click of the lock turning.

I turn towards the door just as it opens.

Addison.

I push forward, excitement beating at me.

Addison.

ADDISON

I watch with bated breath as Melchior walks out of the cell, his gait determined.

I want to run up to him immediately, but Drosdan told me to hang back for a bit, to give Melchior a wide berth as he recovers from being trapped in the bijass. I resist the urge to go to him despite how much I want to.

I search his face, trying to gauge his state. That moment of clarity I saw earlier has faded, but not completely.

And as I watch him, every part of me attuned to him, I see it start to come back again. It takes a moment, but when his eyes lock on mine once more...I know he's fully back. I can see him in there.

He stares right through me, all of his faculties back on line—and then some. I can feel him at the edge of my consciousness, a strong and steady presence. And maybe I'm wrong, but I feel like he understands everything, all of what happened between us and accepts me anyway.

I swallow, my throat clicking passed the nervous dryness. "I'm sorry," I whisper, my voice coming out hoarse. "Melchior...I'm sorry." I pour all of myself into those two words.

Not the apology that I expected to give him when I had the chance once more, but it's what comes out right then. And he doesn't reject it, though I might not blame him if he did.

Instead, he inclines his head, his eyes not leaving my own.

Cool relief flows through me at his acceptance.

I can't stay this far away from him a second longer. I close the distance between us. I know Drosdan is still there, watching, but he's almost a part of the background as I take Melchior's large hand in mine.

I only have eyes for him. He's all that exists for me right then.

But I want him alone. I don't want even a passive audience to this very private moment.

When I turn and tug him along, he follows easily. Drosdan doesn't object. Even he can see that Melchior is fully in control, that he won't hurt me or anyone else.

I lead him directly to the cave I've been using when I come to visit. I need time alone with him, time to connect, time to absorb that he's with me once more.

But once we're there, once we're alone together, Melchior takes the lead. He stops me, his fully lucid gaze meeting my own. Wrapping an arm around my waist, he pulls me down gently, lying down with me on the pallet already set up on the ground.

He still doesn't speak a word to me as he sets his mouth against mine, but he says so much with his touch alone.

I sigh, kissing him back, wrapping my arms around his neck, pressing my body against his solidness. A tear escapes and trickles down my temple. It's so good to have him back in my arms, so good to feel him against me. He breaks the kiss, his eyes soft as he wipes at mine. He doesn't cry. The Zmaj are built to conserve water. But I can see how full of emotion his gaze is all the same.

He reaches for my clothes, his hands gentle, reverent as

he takes them off, kissing every inch of skin as it's revealed. I hum at the touch. It means so much. When he gets to the stitches that had to ultimately be placed along the deeper wounds along my side, he hesitates.

I have a moment where I'm afraid it'll trigger the bijass once more, take him back to that initial point during that battle that sent him over the edge.

But after that brief stillness, he just lowers his head and kisses the stitches softly, his touch even more gentle now.

Sighing, I relax back on the pallet, closing my eyes to enjoy the gentle touches, the soft kisses he lays on me. He moves down my body, kissing my hip, the length of my legs, even the soles of my feet. When he starts to make his way back up the inside of my thigh, I let my legs fall open.

Yes.

I want him everywhere.

He lavishes my core with the same slow patience, the same delicate touch, until my eyes are squeezed tightly shut, my hands clenched in his hair. I'm so close I can almost taste it, that delicious edge of pleasure just out of reach.

But I stop him.

This isn't how I want to get there.

Not this first time.

That's how it feels. Like we're having our first time all over again. He lifts his head when I tug at his hair, his gaze confused.

"I want to have you inside me," I murmur, tugging him up.

His face clears as he allows me to do so, helping me with his clothes. Once they're off, I can't help sliding my hands over all of that smooth skin, the soft scales, his wings...

I kiss my way down the strong column of his neck, down to his chest to nuzzle at the tightness of his nipples, past his chiseled abs that are somehow even more chiseled now after being locked up.

My hands settle on the thick muscle of his thighs, and I look up to meet his heated gaze. He watches me intently. I lean down to kiss the thick length of his erection, not breaking that intimate stare. It jumps at the touch.

Mmm.

Taking the base in my hand, I lift it up off his stomach and take it into my mouth, enjoying the way his entire body stiffens at the touch. Enjoying the power I have over him. I swirl my tongue over the head before taking him in deeper, enjoying the heft, the silky skin. I could touch him just like this for hours, watch the play of expressions across his face as he enjoys each touch.

I forget that I want him inside me, enjoying that moment too much, wanting to lavish attention on him—but he doesn't forget. When his thighs start to tremble under me, he reaches down to lift me off of him gently. I let him. Fair's fair after all, and I know I want what he does.

But he doesn't flip us over so I'm on the bottom, like I half-expect him to. He stays on his back and arranges me over him, spreading my legs over his erection. I bite my lip. Using one hand to brace myself against his hard chest and the other to grip him, I point him up towards my entrance. I'm so wet that I can feel it sliding down my thigh.

I still feel a hint of trepidation as the thick head touches me. It's been a few days since we've done this and it's always a tight fit. Melchior's hands tighten on my hips as I slowly push down onto him, my eyes automatically closing as I stretch around his girth.

Melchior's hand slides around my hip and to the inside of my thigh, his fingers finding my clitoris, already swollen and sensitive from his mouth.

I sigh as I lift up and push back down again, his fingers working their knowing magic. He knows just how I like to be touched now. Knows me better than anyone ever has.

It takes some work to get him in all the way, but I finally do, both of us moaning as I settle onto his hips. I feel so completely full of him, and I love it.

Opening my eyes, I brace myself on his chest and start to work myself on him, my eyes meeting his in the dim light. I keep the rhythm slow, enjoying every inch that slides in and then back out of me. I lower myself to my forearms on his chest, sharing a soft, clinging kiss with Melchior. With my mate. Even just thinking the word results in a burst of joy in my own chest.

My mate.

Melchior is my mate. I relish the word as my tongue tangles with his, as his length throbs inside me. As his consciousness flirts with my own, a warmth around the outskirts of my awareness.

It might sound crazy later or it might not, but I know we're connected beyond what I would have ever thought possible during my days on the ship. We're as close as two people can get. And I wouldn't want it any other way.

I break the kiss, my lips just barely brushing his as I continue to move on him, our bodies skimming against each other as I do. The ridges on his cock... My eyes almost cross as they continue to hit me just right. My movements start to lose their smoothness as I speed up, the climax building once more. Melchior tilts his head, kissing the side of my neck, my shoulder, my collarbone, his hands cupping my butt and steadying me as I move on him.

Almost...

Everything feels so good, so perfect after so much time apart...

Crying out, I stiffen above him, burying my face against his shoulder as the orgasm tears through me, my body shuddering at the pleasure.

Melchior groans underneath me, his hands tightening on

my backside, his hips pumping up into me. I feel his orgasm hit him directly on the heels of my own, his body trembling against mine. I lift my head so I can see his face, his eyes, my own half-closed from my own climax.

He reaches up to cup my face with his hands, laying a gentle kiss on my lips. His eyes are so full of love they make my breath catch.

"Forever," he whispers, his lips brushing my own with the word.

I feel my heart swell in my chest at the word. Yes.

"Forever," I agree, dropping my forehead against his.

I've never meant anything more.

19

ADDISON

*A*fter declaring Melchior as my mate, he decided that
we need to have a mating ceremony. I'm not really
the type to want to stand up in front everyone, have their
eyes on me while I celebrate something so personal, but I'm
willing to do it for him. And maybe there is something nice
about the formality of it. The commitment of a public celebration. Then when Padraig and Maeve and Fallon and
Arawn suggest we do a tri-ceremony all together, I breathe a
sigh of relief. That's more people to take some of that attention, which is more than fine with me.

On top of that, when Visidion and Rosalind get wind of
our plans, they're fully on board.

"A large celebration, a reason to be happy, to dress up and
blow off steam—it's a good idea," Rosalind says, looking at
each of us in turn. "Something positive to offset all the
negative."

I can see that.

"And we can invite people from all the territories—the
Tribe, the city, and the mining settlement," Visidion adds.

"That's an excellent idea," Rosalind agrees, smiling up at

him where he stands beside her chair. "It will be a good way to build relationships. Formal agreements are great, but they can't take the place of personal links."

He nods, looking at Melchior.

"I like the message this sends. That we will continue to live our lives, that the invaders will not take that from us. That we won't give them that power over us."

It's a sobering yet accurate picture of what's going on, and it makes me feel even better about the ceremony. The meeting doesn't last much longer after that, our piece said.

The communal meal that night has a celebratory air in and of itself, the news of another mating—another three matings—lifting everyone's spirits. I don't mind the congratulations I receive, not when everyone needs something good to focus on.

For once, I even decide to put off tinkering with the invader ship for the night, happy to spend the night with by mate by my side. Walking together into the future, entering that next phase of life.

I tighten my grip on Melchior's hand and he looks down to meet my eyes with a smile as we walk through the tables filled with people enjoying their food.

Melchior has my heart, fully and completely. And for once, I'm not afraid. I don't want to retreat into my shielded solitude. I trust him. I trust myself.

This entire experience, this relationship, has helped me reclaim that small piece of myself that I nearly lost because I was so afraid of being vulnerable. So ready to suppress any part of me that might lead to any kind of unfamiliar territory, any place that I do not have guaranteed control over.

As we get food and take a couple of empty seats, I revel in the normality of it all. I didn't realize how much I would enjoy the little things about being part of a couple. Like always having someone by my side when I want him...it's nice.

Melchior's hand stays in my own as he starts to eat. I look down at our clasped hands, feeling misty-eyed about everything. I never thought I would ever be this sappy person. But with Melchior...I really am. I can't help it.

"Is something wrong?"

I look up at his concerned murmur, meeting those gorgeous eyes. Eyes that I'm going to see looking back at me every morning from here on out. And isn't that just great?

"No," I reassure him, leaning into him to kiss his cheek. Any reservations I had about being public about our relationship seem silly now. I'm not that frightened, insecure person anymore. "I love you."

The concern melts away into a look that I know I will always treasure.

"I love you too," he says, raising my hand and kissing the back of it.

I sigh, completely content as I lean into his side.

Love was there all along.

I just had to be brave enough to reach for it.

EPILOGUE

MELCHIOR

*W*e come across the invader in a grouping of rocks not far from the city, lurking in the shadows. A spy? A scout? It is not clear. There are too many things off for either of those to fit perfectly.

For one, he is not wearing the carapace armor his comrades always have on.

For another, he is alone. We have never come across any of the invaders alone before.

The last clue that points to a different story altogether are the remnants of restraints on both of his ankles. The metal chain attaching one to the other to hobble him was obviously broken using crude tools. Perhaps rocks, as those are in abundance in this particular area.

In any case, we decide to take him in to see Rosalind and Visidion. Curiously, the invader does not seem to try too hard to escape.

Bystanders take a step back as we march him through the city to Rosalind's office. I understand. The only invaders we have brought into the city to date have not been breathing, let alone walking on their own two feet.

Rosalind waves us in immediately.

"What is this?" Visidion demands, looking the invader over.

"We found him in one of the groupings of rocks nearby," I explain. "Alone." I point at the remnants of his restraints. "He did not resist much when we took him. Perhaps he was a captive himself?"

"Hmm." Rosalind stands, looking the alien over. He—it? —stands still, looking back. "No armor. Alone. Old restraints. Perhaps he didn't fight you too much because he knew he would die out in the desert alone."

That is a sound theory.

"We are not here to save invaders, be they prisoners or attackers," Visidion says coldly.

"Perhaps," Rosalind returns mildly, staring. "On the other hand, perhaps this is an opportunity."

"An opportunity?" Visidion asks incredulously.

"Yes." She looks beyond us to the door, where her assistant hovers. "Can you please bring the scientific team here?"

"Yes, of course."

Addison.

I feel a rush of anticipation even though we spend much of our time together now. I do not think that rush will ever truly go away. I love spending time with my mate.

It does not take long for the assistant to return with Errol and Addison. Addison's eyes find me immediately, and she smiles, moving towards me, but then hesitates when her eyes fall upon the invader. Her face pales, and I know she is remembering her own encounter with the invaders. The wounds have still not fully healed.

I want to go to her but remain in place. I must ensure our prisoner does not do any harm.

"Errol, Addison—do you think you could glean some

useful knowledge from having this invader to observe and test?"

Errol and Addison glance at each other.

"Perhaps," Errol says cautiously. "But, why...?"

"We found him alone, without armor, and with the remnants of restraints," I explain. "He could have been a captive himself."

Or he could be a spy. A trap. I know we are all thinking the same.

"Oh," Addison murmurs, her gaze lighting with curiosity. She always has an abundance of it—one of the traits that makes her so good at what she does. "It would be interesting to learn more about them. Bodies are all well and good, but it's not the same as a live being."

"Excellent," Rosalind says, nodding decisively. "The scientific team may take him for research. I will assign two guards to him at all times. But I still urge you to take care."

I frown, but do not interject. I do not like the idea of Addison near a live invader, even with guards, but I do not voice that concern. I know it is not a completely rational one in this instance. But I will watch. If the invader does something even slightly suspicious around Addison... I will not ask it to clarify its intentions.

"You are all dismissed," Rosalind announces, sitting back down. "Thank you."

I hope this is not a mistake.

THE END

ABOUT THE AUTHOR

USA Today Bestselling Author of fantasy and scifi romance, Miranda Martin's books feature larger than life heroes with out-of-this-world anatomy and smart heroines destined to save the world. As a little girl she would sneak off with her nose in a book, dreaming of magical realms. Today she brings those fantasies to life and adores every fan who chooses to live in them for a while.

She was born and raised in southern Virginia, but as a veteran she's traveled to places like Korea, Hawaii and good 'ole Texas. Now she's settled in Kansas, the heart of America, with her husband and daughters. Her favorite animals are dragons, unicorns and cats. If she's not writing, you can still find her tucked away somewhere with a warm blanket and her nose in a book.

Get in touch!
mirandamartinromance.com
miranda@mirandamartinromance.com

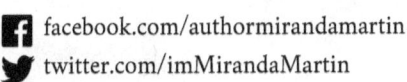

facebook.com/authormirandamartin
twitter.com/imMirandaMartin
instagram.com/imMirandaMartin